Sebastian's Fate

Etherya's Earth, Book 7.5

By

REBECCA HEFNER

Contents

Cover Design: Anthony O'Brien, BookCoverDesign.store
Proofreading and Editing: Bryony Leah, www.bryonyleah.com

For Julie Burns and all the readers who asked for Celine and Sebastian's story after reading **Garridan's Mate.** I never expected so many people to want their story, and I'm thrilled to bring it to you. Thanks to all of you who love Etherya's Earth as much as I do!

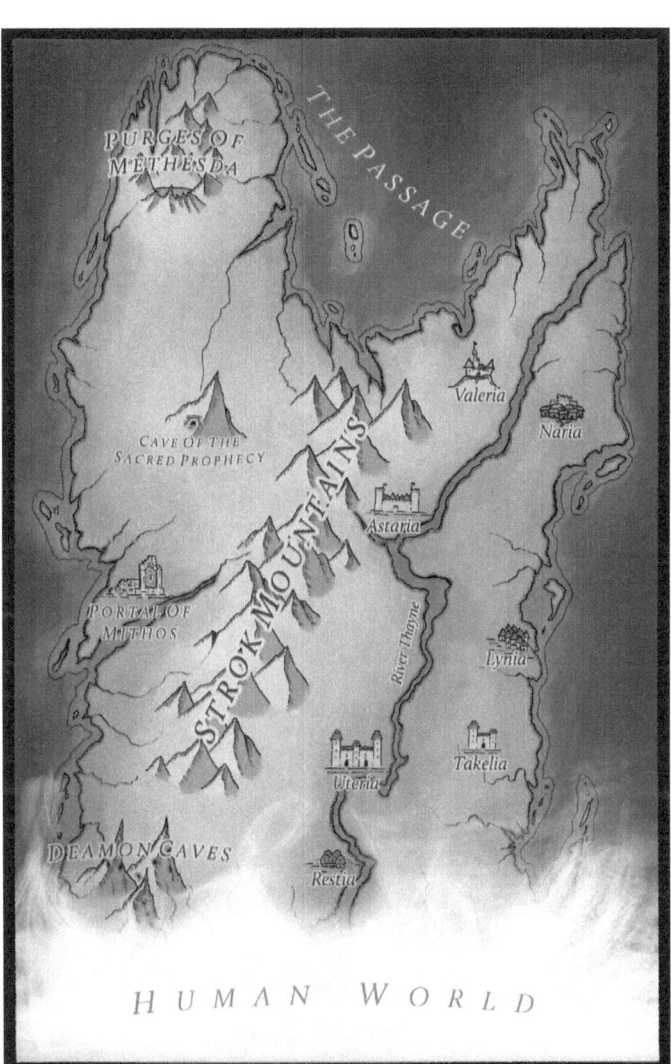

Chapter 1

S ebastian, son of Astaroth, sat at his desk in the governor's mansion at Valeria angrily shuffling papers. Muttering as he found the document he needed, he shoved the rest away so he could concentrate. Narrowing his eyes, he read the decree from Queen Miranda and King Sathan:

To the Esteemed Governors and council members of the immortal realm:

In honor of the destruction of the ether and the imminent immersion with humans, it is imperative we learn the basics of their most popular traditions. As Prince Tordor and Princess Esme continue to slowly integrate the species, we feel it is important to become educated on their common practices.

One of the most important human holidays is Christmas, so this year we have chosen Valeria to hold a Christmas celebration for the realm. Any immortal is welcome to join and learn about the holiday, and Prince Heden's wife, Sofia, will be in attendance to help.

Although many revere Etherya in our realm and we encourage her worship, we see the benefit of learning about our new neighbors on the Earth. Etherya has given King Sathan her blessing to hold the Christmas festivities, and we hope you find them educational and enjoyable.

As always, we are your humble rulers and encourage anyone to contact us with questions.

Sincerely.

Queen Miranda and King Sathan

Swiping a hand over his face, Sebastian swore and reached for a blank piece of paper. He began to scrawl notes, reminding himself there was still much to do before next week's Christmas celebration.

The festivity would last several days, culminating in a lavish banquet to be held on the final night. A huge team had already been dispatched to cover Valeria's main square with Christmas-themed decorations, and he'd noticed the tinsel-wrapped streetlamps and poinsettia plants lining the street on his walk to the governor's mansion earlier that morning.

Sebastian only lived a few blocks from the mansion—a renovated castle that had resided in the center of the Valerian compound for centuries. Governor Camron lived there with his family, but it also held the council offices. It was close to Sebastian's home, so he usually walked to work. As the head of the Valerian council, he took his job seriously and was always early. He'd worked hard to become the youngest council leader in Vampyre history and was determined to prove his worth.

Even if he had to plan a four-day celebration for a human holiday he knew nothing about.

Gritting his teeth, he scowled when his friend Mila breezed into the room.

"Well, don't you look like you've been run over by a four-wheeler?" she chided, plopping into one of the leather chairs that faced his desk. Reaching over to the bowl that held fresh apples, she snagged one and bit off a huge chunk.

"Nice to see you too," he droned, "and please, help yourself."

"Thanks." Gesturing to his desk with the hand that held the apple, she squinted. "Still drowning in administrative crap for the Christmas celebration? Why don't you have Camron help you?"

"Camron is busy with the governor's duties, and as head of the council, it's a good way to show the older members I'm deserving of the title they all secretly crave."

"Still trying to prove you're the best," she said, taking another bite, her jaw working as she chewed. "Do you think one day you might actually believe it? You're the only one who still needs convincing. Everybody else respects you, Sebastian. Maybe it's time you took a *tiny* break and had some fun." She held her thumb and forefinger an inch apart. "Look at Garridan. He's head over heels for Siora, and I've never seen him happier. Maybe getting laid would take that scowl off your face too."

Shooting her a glare, Sebastian waited several seconds for effect before speaking. "I have no desire to get laid or spend time with any woman at the moment. I'm drowning in work here." He waved his hand over the multitude of paperwork. "On that note, I need your help."

"Oh no," she said, sitting up and tossing her apple in the nearby trash can. "I'm not going as your date to the gala. We've used each other as fake dates for long enough, and I'm ready to play the field a little."

Lifting his brows, he grinned. "No way. Mila, the staunch, independent woman, finally wants to find a mate?"

"*Mate* might be a stretch," she said, scrunching her features, "but the kingdom has evolved far enough that I can at least try." Her lips curved. "Queen Miranda, Governor Evie, and Princess Arderin have ushered in a new era for this realm, and I can finally hold my head high like the lesbian Vampyre I am and date who I want."

"Wow," he said, sitting back and rubbing his chin. "I'm proud to hear you say that, Mila. I've always respected who you are and hated you had to hide your true nature."

"You and Garridan have always accepted me even if the other stuffy aristocrats don't. I'm thankful for you both."

"But not enough to be my fake date to the Christmas gala."

Chuckling, she shook her head. "I can't keep being your fallback, Sebastian. I need to get out there, and you do too. It's time you found something else to focus on besides work."

"I like my work," he said, forming a small pout.

"And you're an excellent council leader, but you deserve companionship, and yes, I think you deserve some really good sex too."

Pursing his lips, he considered her words. "It *has* been a long time, but I don't even know where to start. You know I detest the aristocratic women Father wants me to date. They're all so vapid and boring."

"Well, I hate to break it to you, but you're an aristocrat too, so maybe *you're* boring."

Glancing at the mound of work on his desk, he breathed a laugh. "I want to argue with you, but you might be right. Regardless, I have no desire to date. If you won't go as my fake date, the least you can do is help me find someone else. You do run a matchmaking agency after all."

Mila had opened the matchmaking agency a year ago with tremendous success. Many Vampyres, Slayers, and reformed Deamons had found love through her services. Pride swelled in his chest that his friend had triumphed doing something she enjoyed.

"Yes, but all my clients *want* to fall in love. I can't set them up with someone who doesn't want a relationship."

"The Christmas gala is a masked formal affair. I won't even have to see the woman's face, for the goddess's sake, and she won't have to see mine. It can be a hands-off business transaction that will only last a few hours. If you can find an amenable client, tell her I'll purchase drinks for her all night and leave a gift certificate for five thousand lira in her name at the boutique in the main square." He pointed out the window to the sprawling street that led to the main square. "That should do it."

"You want to pay one of my clients to be your date?" Mila asked incredulously. "Come on, Sebastian. You're a good-looking guy with that mop of thick brown hair and those chocolate-brown eyes. Plus, I bet most women would think your fangs were cute if you ever smiled."

"I smile," he said, discounting the statement as he frowned.

"Rarely," was her sardonic response. "But seriously, if you put in a little effort, I'm sure you can find a date."

"I don't want the hassle," he said, shaking his head. "Please do this for me, Mila."

Rising, she placed her fist on her hip. "You're a pain in my ass, you know that?"

Chuckling, he stood and walked around the desk to gently grip her upper arms. "Just think about it, okay? Look through your client list and see if there's someone amenable. I'm sure there's a woman who needs some new fancy dresses. There always are on this stuffy compound."

Squinting one eye, she studied him. "Fine. I'll look through my list, but I don't think I'm going to find any—"

"Perfect," he said, turning and urging her toward the door. "I'm sure if you look hard enough you'll find the right woman." Gesturing across the threshold, he gave a slight bow. "I have faith in you, Mila. Now, let me get back to work. I have way too much to do and barely any time left to do it."

"One day, I'm going to find a mate for you out of sheer spite," she said, cocking a brow. "The work is always going to be there, Sebastian. You need to live a little—"

"Bye for now!" he interjected, waving and closing the door in her face.

"Hope you get a thousand papercuts!" she teased through the door.

Laughing, he strode back to the desk ready to finish the last of the planning so he could begin the final phase of ensuring everything was perfect. Hoping like hell Mila would take his request seriously, he didn't give any more thought to finding a date. No—Mila would come through for him, allowing him to mark that chore off his list.

Chapter 2

C eline, daughter of Handor, stood atop the ladder in her sprawling back yard, reaching for the juicy peach that was just out of reach. Her father had instructed their landscapers to plant a row of peach trees several years ago, and she loved the succulent fruit. Although Vampyres only needed Slayer blood for sustenance, they still ate food for pleasure.

Grunting, she reached further, gasping with excitement when she clutched the fruit. Tugging it from the branch, she wobbled on the ladder before slowly climbing down. Thrilled with her successful conquest, she sat on the soft grass and brushed the skin of the fruit with her hands. Satisfied, she took a bite and slowly chewed, savoring the taste.

"Look at you out here picking fruit like a laborer," Mila called as she approached. "Handor would have a fit."

"We all know I'm his favorite since I'm the only girl," was her cheeky reply as she took another bite. Swallowing, she grinned when Mila sat beside her. "Three brothers, but I'm the baby girl. What can I say?"

Chuckling, Mila rested her forearms on her bent knees. "Everyone underestimates you, Celine. It's a damn tragedy. They all think you're just some vapid aristocrat with a pretty face, but you're always plotting under all that beauty." She circled her hand over her face. "It's not fair to the rest of us normal-looking immortals."

Sighing, Celine leaned back, resting on her palm as she gazed over the rolling hills. "What does it matter anyway? No one seems to notice me in this stupid kingdom, and I might as well be an old spinster at this point."

"I think most men are intimidated by your wealth and looks—"

"I'm not wealthy," she said, lifting a finger. "My father is."

"True, but you're his responsibility until you find a mate and bond. So, technically, you're wealthy too."

"I guess." Sliding her hand over the soft grass, she frowned. "It also doesn't help that I'm determined to catch the eye of someone who doesn't even know I exist."

"Ah, Sebastian," Mila said, stretching out her legs and crossing one over the other. "He's determined not to notice *any* woman, believe me. I just had the most annoying conversation with him."

Celine's ears perked at the mention of the man she was slightly obsessed with—and who barely ever acknowledged her. "Do tell," she said, trying not to sound too interested.

"You know we always take each other as dates to the stupid galas we hate, but I want to attend the Christmas gala solo. There are a few ladies I have my eye on, and I don't want to squander the opportunity to secure some one-on-one time with them. Being by Sebastian's side isn't going to cut it."

"Oh," Celine said, trying to tamp down her excitement that he needed a date. Was there some way she could maneuver herself into the position? "That's lovely, Mila. I want you to find love."

"I want you to find love too, but you insist on pining for a man who isn't interested in anything but his council position."

"I've tried to get him to notice me so many times," Celine said wistfully, glancing down at the functional clothes she'd worn to pick fruit. "I never wear anything like this when I know he's going to be near. I always put my best foot forward, make sure my gown and makeup are perfect, and he still doesn't have a clue I'm alive."

"He's an idiot, Celine," Mila said, shrugging. "Most men are."

"Garridan even tried to help me. He thinks I'd be a good match for his brother. Remember when he took me to the fundraiser? We tried to make Sebastian jealous, but he only stayed for an hour and then went downstairs to his office to work."

"He's married to his job and too stubborn to open himself up to meeting a mate. It's no way to live, but you can't help someone who doesn't want to change."

Celine's eyebrows drew together. "Why was your conversation with him annoying?"

"Because he wants me to set him up with one of my clients for the Christmas gala."

"Oh..." Swallowing thickly, Celine tried to tamp down the jealousy that immediately swelled at the thought of him taking someone else. "What did you say?"

"No, of course," Mila said, bristling. "My clients want a relationship, and he doesn't. It wouldn't be fair to them."

"I wish my father would let me sign up for your matchmaking service. He says it's beneath my station."

"My dear," Mila said, leaning closer, "your father is a stick in the mud."

Tossing back her head, she laughed. "I guess he is. He's consumed with tradition and proper etiquette, but he tries. Still, I might wither away if I don't employ *some* new tactics to find a mate." Lifting her gaze to Mila's, Celine slowly cocked her eyebrow.

"Oh, no," Mila said, showing her palms. "I'm not falling for that. I can't set you up with Sebastian. You remember what he said to me, right?"

Her lips formed a pout as she nodded. "He told you he wasn't interested in me and thinks I would've been a better match for Garridan." Glancing over, she said, "Which isn't true. Obviously, Siora is Garridan's perfect mate."

"Sebastian is a proud man, Celine. Rumors were rampant about your possible betrothal to Garridan, so he'll never see you as a viable option. He doesn't want to be seen as the man who ended up with a woman his brother didn't choose. It's completely ridiculous, but he's hardheaded."

"Men," Celine huffed, cocking her arm before tossing the peach far into the meadow. "Screw him and his stupid pride. If he'd just be open, I could show him I'm not the bumbling idiot he thinks I am."

"I want you to be happy, Celine, but he might not be worthy of you. Perhaps there's someone better-suited for you out there. You'll never know unless you release this infatuation with a man who doesn't want you back." Covering her hand, she squeezed. "I'm not trying to be harsh, but I want the best for you."

Inhaling the fragrant air, Celine stared toward the horizon, wishing with all her might she could be open to someone else. It would be infinitely easier to focus on someone who actually *liked* her and didn't see her as a boring, empty-headed aristocrat.

Unfortunately, she was rather consumed with Sebastian. His broad shoulders, thick hair, and deep brown eyes should've appeared quite normal, but to her, they were gorgeous. His features were austere and aristocratic, and she often daydreamed about lying in his arms and trailing her finger down his nose. It may seem silly to others, but she craved that intimacy with a mate...with *him*.

Many across the kingdom saw Sebastian as rigid and unyielding, consumed with his council position. They'd never seen him as she had, when no one was watching. Celine loved to walk through the manicured neighborhoods of Valeria and often strolled by Sebastian's home. He still lived in his parents' house, as most aristocrats did until they bonded and had families, and she would observe him doing chores in the back yard as she strolled by.

Many aristocratic men would hire others to perform the duties, but she'd overheard Sebastian tell Garridan once that doing the menial tasks allowed him to release some steam and maintain his physique. Garridan had mumbled something about him needing to get laid, which had promptly caused her cheeks to flush and she'd rushed away, ashamed she was eavesdropping.

During her walks, Celine had observed him tackling many tasks. There were the times when he would chop wood, his skin glistening in the sun as rivulets of sweat ran down his chest between the spiky dark hairs. How would it feel to lick away the wetness? To drag her tongue over his copper-colored nipple as she gazed into his fathomless eyes?

"Earth to Celine," Mila interrupted, snapping her fingers. "Where did you go?"

"Just daydreaming," was her wistful reply as she curled her knees into her chest. "Did you know Sebastian chops wood for his parents' fireplace even though they have staff who could do it instead?"

Shooting her a derisive look, Mila droned, "Yeah, he's a saint."

"Oh, stop," Celine said, swatting her arm. "He also helped the little girl who lives next to them train all three of her puppies. He would get up early each morning and help Chandra before he went to work."

"That's nice to know, creepy stalker," Mila teased, leaning back on her palms. "Tell me more."

Ignoring her dismissive tone, Celine continued. "He also offered to hold Lila's literacy group sessions in his back yard when the governor's mansion was being renovated and the meeting rooms weren't available. Not only did he provide the space, but he helped teach the citizens to read."

"He's a council member. Maybe it was just to get in Lila's good graces. She *is* bonded to the king's brother after all."

"Goddess, you're cynical." Celine wrinkled her nose. "I think he's a genuine person who excels at his council job so he can prove to the world he's worthy. Being the oldest son carries great pressure. Xandor speaks about it often," she said, referencing her eldest brother.

"I actually said something similar to him earlier," Mila agreed, rubbing the back of her neck. "Maybe he is all gooey inside and just needs something to shake up his regimented demeanor so he'll stop working so much."

"You want to know the sweetest thing?" Celine asked, leaning forward as if imparting words of great importance.

Mila's eyebrows lifted as she nodded.

"One day when he was chopping wood, there were these two chipmunks who kept circling the stump. Instead of shooing them away, he picked up one of the leaves that had fallen from the nearby tree and fashioned it into a bowl. He poured some water from his canister into the leaf so they'd have fresh water to drink. Isn't that thoughtful?"

Glancing toward the sky, Mila rolled her eyes. "Goddess, please help my friend before she swoons to death."

"Oh, forget it," Celine said, stomping her foot in the grass. "I'm sorry I told you. I just think it's sweet."

Mila considered her for a moment before speaking. "Wow, you've got it bad for him. I wish things were different for you, Celine. I really do."

Turning to face her, Celine gently gripped her forearm. "Then let me go as his date to the Christmas gala."

Confusion entered her eyes. "I can't. He'll never agree to have you as his date. You may think he's Prince Charming, but he's made up his mind about you, Celine."

"Then don't tell him it's me."

Mila's mouth fell open, and she worked her jaw as she appeared baffled. "Um, that would be great, but you two have known each other forever. Not quite sure how—"

"I have a plan," Celine said with a confident nod. "You'll tell Sebastian that one of your clients agreed to be his 'business' date." She made quotation marks with her fingers.

"But it will be you?"

"Yes," Celine said, excitement blooming in her chest. "It's a masked gala, so I'll wear a mask the entire time, and also a wig." Pointing to her long blond hair, she lifted a shoulder. "I've always thought I'd look pretty good with black hair. This is a perfect time to try."

"You'd look great in a paper bag, Celine," Mila muttered, features scrunching as she considered her plan. "I think you're the most beautiful woman on the compound. But even if you wear a wig and a mask he'll see your eyes."

"Oh, eighty percent of Vampyres in the kingdom have ice-blue eyes. Since they're not rare, I'll be fine."

Tilting her head, Mila studied her. "Your eyes are still unique, Celine. Everyone's are. Windows into the soul and that whole thing."

With a harumph, Celine crossed her arms. "It's not like Sebastian has ever even looked me in the eye, so that's a moot point. He won't suspect a thing, trust me. He thinks I'm some timid wallflower content to drink tea and die of boredom each day."

Amusement, along with a faint glint of respect, lit Mila's eyes. "Damn, this plan is kind of badass. I admit I didn't expect it from you."

"Look, I know what people think of me, and I can only live the life I've known. Yes, I'm an aristocrat and I do my best to make my parents proud, but deep inside, I long to be so much more. This will allow me to explore being someone else for a night. It's so exciting!"

"And if he falls for it?" Mila asked, cupping Celine's shoulder. "What will you do then? What if he wants to kiss you? Or more?"

Wrinkling her nose, Celine pondered. "Well, I would certainly kiss him back. Goddess knows I've dreamed of it about a million times."

"And your virginity? What if he wants to go further?"

"Ah, yes, my aristocratic virginity that I must hold intact until I bond." Sighing, she plucked the grass as she spoke. "It's so stupid. I wish I were more experienced so I could please him..."

"Celine, giving your virginity to someone is a huge deal. Hell, I'm still a virgin too. You can't do that while you pretend to be someone else. It's not you."

Staring at the ground, Celine contemplated the words. "Maybe I could or maybe not. I won't know until I'm in the heat of the moment, I guess."

They sat for a moment considering all the outcomes—both successful and disastrous—before Mila finally spoke.

"It's crazy, Celine. The whole hair-brained scheme." Her lips curved into a mischievous grin. "But honestly, Sebastian could use some excitement in his life, and you could too." Gnawing her lip, she mulled over the details. "I can't believe I'm going to say this, but..." she waggled her eyebrows. "I think we should do it."

"Yeah?" Celine asked, trying not to give in to the urge to break into cartwheels on the open field.

"Yes," she said, facing her and crossing her legs. "I'll tell Sebastian I found a client named..."

"Anya," Celine said, eyes widening with eagerness. "I've always thought that name was so sexy. *Kiss me, Anya...*" she said in a deep voice, mimicking Sebastian's.

"Oh, brother," Mila said, rolling her eyes. "Okay, *Anya*, I'll set you up with Sebastian. But if he figures it out, I'm going to tell him it was your idea."

"Thank you, thank you, thank you!" Celine said, throwing her arms around her friend and hugging for dear life. "This is amazing. I'm finally going on a date with Sebastian!"

"No," Mila said, drawing back, "*Anya* is."

"Oh, whatever," she said, waving a dismissive hand. "I'll know it's me and that will be amazing."

"Celine," Mila said, taking her hands and squeezing affectionately. "This might not change anything. It might just be one night and you'll return to your regular lives afterward. I don't want you to be disappointed."

"I know," she said, nodding. "But maybe it will help me build my confidence at least. If he shows any sign of attraction to me, perhaps I can begin to believe *someone* will want to bond with me, even if it isn't him."

"You deserve to hold every confidence, Celine. You're beautiful, smart, and very strong-willed although your father hides you in a gilded cage. As I said, I think the men of this kingdom are idiots who are either too intimidated or too stupid to see your true brilliance. You're so much more than Handor's daughter."

"Thank you." Celine shook Mila's hands, gripping them by the wrists as they held each other. Mila had been her friend for many years, and she was grateful to have her in her sometimes sheltered life. "You deserve the same, Mila. I hope you find love one day."

"From your lips to the goddess's ears," Mila said, pointing to the sky. "I'll call Sebastian later today and give him the good news." Arching a brow, she muttered, "At least, I *think* it's good news."

Laughing, Celine rose, helping Mila stand before throwing an arm over her shoulders. "You'll see," she said as they began to stroll back to the house. "It's going to be fun."

They reached the front gate and Mila stepped onto the sidewalk. "Glad I saw you back there as I was walking to the office," she said, giving a salute. "It certainly was an interesting detour. I'll let you know what Sebastian says."

"You're the best, Mila!" Celine called as she trailed away.

Her friend lifted her arm, waving as she continued toward her matchmaking agency.

Emitting a tiny squeal, Celine clenched her hands in front of her chest, praying to the goddess she hadn't made a mistake.

Chapter 3

S ebastian received the call from Mila as he was walking home later that evening. Lifting the phone to his ear, he grinned.

"Tell me some good news."

"You'll never believe this, but I found a woman willing to put up with you—for one night at least."

Chuckling, he slipped his hand into his pants pocket, happy she'd found a "date" for him. "Who is she? Anyone I know?"

"Nope. Her name is Anya and she requested to stay anonymous."

"Anonymous...how?"

"She agreed to be your gala date, but she wants to keep the mask on the whole time. It's the only way she'll attend."

Kicking a pebble in his path, he frowned as curiosity and a slight bit of disappointment welled within.

"Is this personal? How can a woman I've never met hate me?"

"So he does have a heart," Mila murmured, causing him to scowl. "It's not personal, Sebastian. She lives at Astaria and has never heard of you. You have a clean slate. Don't fuck it up."

Relief coursed through him. "Okay. Is it strange to say I'm slightly excited to meet this mystery woman?"

"Not at all. I'm thrilled you're excited at the possibility of dating. Maybe after you and 'mystery girl' finish your date, you can focus on someone you actually have a chance with. Celine maybe?"

Sighing, he shook his head. "We've been over this, Mila. Celine is lovely but reminds me of a porcelain doll. She's the embodiment of 'seen and not heard.' I don't think I've ever heard her utter more than five words."

"Um, it's hard to speak to someone who rarely exists outside of his office. And have you ever tried to speak to her? You might be surprised."

"Look, I know you two are good friends, although I can't fathom what someone with your gregarious personality talks about with someone as mousy as Celine."

Her laugh wafted over the phone, causing him to scowl.

"What the hell are you laughing at?"

"You. I don't even feel bad anymore. I did for a while, but you deserve what's coming to you."

Baffled, Sebastian harshly rubbed his forehead. "I have no idea what the hell you're talking about."

"Oh, you will," she said, her tone mischievous. "Anyway, Anya will meet you promptly at seven in front of Lady Anne's Boutique in the main square. She's going to take you up on your offer to buy her a plethora of fancy gowns."

"Fine with me."

"You have to wear your mask the entire time, and she hers. That's the deal. Are we clear, Sebastian?"

"Crystal. Thanks for doing this, Mila. I owe you one."

"Just have fun and keep an open mind, okay?"

"I always keep an open mind," he said with a small pout.

The infuriating woman laughed so hard she snorted. Annoyed, he waited for the guffaws to abate.

"Are you finished?" he droned.

"Sorry, the 'open mind' thing threw me for a second. Have a good night, Sebastian. See you at the gala."

"See you there. Thanks again, Mila."

Clicking off the phone, he continued home as curiosity about his upcoming mystery date welled deep within.

"**W**ell, he's as happy as a clam." Mila's voice chimed over the phone as Celine sat on her bed painting her toenails. The phone was on speaker where it sat on her comforter, and she grinned as she drew the tiny brush over her pinkie toenail.

"He doesn't suspect anything?"

"Nope. I told him you were from Astaria and had never heard of him. So you can't indicate you know anything about him, okay?"

"Got it. I picked out this gorgeous dark green gown that's going to knock his socks off. I figured that fits with the whole Christmas theme, right?"

"Your guess is as good as mine. Who'd have thought we'd ever need to learn about the traditions of human heathens?"

Chuckling, Celine recapped the polish and reached for the clear setting gel. "I think it's exciting. A whole new species we're going to eventually integrate with. It's noble of Tordor and Esme to pave the path for us."

"It is. I mean, he gave up his kingdom to live with her in the human realm and slowly integrate the species. Talk about some true damn love."

Sighing, Celine rested her chin on her upturned knee. "Do you think we'll find it one day, Mila?"

"I sure hope so. On that note, I've got to dig through my closet and find something to wear on

Saturday. It won't be as fancy as your outfit, I'm sure, but I still plan to knock a lady or two's socks off."

"You're going to look beautiful. You're so confident and genuine. It makes you absolutely stunning, Mila."

"Well, thanks for confirming you're the nicest person ever. Give Sebastian hell. He's going to meet you in front of Lady Anne's Boutique in the main square. As payment for your 'service,' he's also going to deposit a five-thousand-lira stipend in Anya's name for you to buy anything your heart desires."

"I don't need anything," Celine said, glancing toward her closet.

"I know, but the slightly twisted part of me makes him want to pay anyway."

Laughing, Celine wiggled her toes as they dried. "You're too much. If he leaves a stipend, I'll just give it to charity. Goddess knows many others need it more than me."

"You're a good egg, Celine. I wish more people knew the real you."

"So do I," was her soft reply as she ruminated on how others in the kingdom saw her. Meek. Biddable. Boring. Perhaps her luck was about to change...even if she were anonymous. "Sweet dreams, Mila. See you Saturday. Or should I say, *Anya* will see you Saturday...?"

Mila's chuckle wafted through the phone. "See you Saturday."

The phone went dark, and Celine plopped back on the bed, her golden hair splaying over the pillow. Yes, Saturday would be here soon enough, and she was determined to show the world she could be someone other than the woman everyone had already decided she was.

Chapter 4

The day of the gala arrived and Celine racked her brain for an acceptable excuse not to accompany her parents and brothers to it. When she didn't have a date for formal events, she always attended with her family. Of course, tonight, that was impossible.

Since Vampyres had self-healing abilities she couldn't feign sickness. But Vampyres still experienced occasional headaches and exhaustion, so she figured she'd use that excuse and hope her father believed her. She rarely missed formal functions since it was important to her father that she represent their family in public. But she also knew her father well, and he detested talking about anything personal—especially when it came to female issues. Snickering, she decided she'd lay it on thick and hope he took the bait.

"Father?" she called, entering his downstairs office.

Looking up from his desk, he smiled under his thick beard. "Hello, sweetheart. I thought you'd be getting ready for the gala."

"About that," she said, resting her hand on her abdomen and splaying it wide. "I was really looking forward to it, but I'm not feeling well."

Narrowing his eyes, he sat back, lacing his fingers behind his head as he studied her. "I'm sure it will pass. These things always do for our kind."

"Normally, I would agree, but you see...well, this is quite embarrassing to tell my father, but it's my time of the month, and my...uh...flow is heavier than normal—"

"For the goddess's sake, Celine," he interjected, scowling as he rested his forearms on the desk. "It's not polite to speak such things aloud."

"I know." Twining her hands in front of her abdomen, she continued, observing him as he grew more uncomfortable by the second. *Perfect.* "Some months are easier than others, but the cramping is terrible, and I fear it will get worse—"

"Fine," he said, holding up a hand and rising. Striding over, he slid his arm across her shoulders. "I can't hear anymore. It's not proper, dear. I'm sorry you're not feeling well. I'll let the royal family know you wished to attend but couldn't." Kissing her forehead, he frowned. "Now, please, no more talk of these private matters, okay?"

"Yes, Father," she said, bowing slightly to hide her grin. "Thank you."

"Feel better, dear." He patted her shoulder, effectively sending her on her way. "I'll tell you all about it tomorrow."

Pivoting, she breezed out of the room, thrilled her plan had worked. She would make sure to avoid her family at the gala since they were the only ones with a chance of recognizing her in her disguise.

Armed with her freedom—for one night at least—she returned to her room, counting the minutes until her family departed so she could head into the balmy night to meet Sebastian.

Sebastian straightened his bow tie in the mirror, ensuring it was perfectly aligned. Checking his cuff links, he took one last look at his reflection before reaching for the mask on his bed. It was white, which complimented his crisp white shirt underneath his tuxedo. Securing the elastic strap behind his head, he maneuvered it around his eyes and over his cheeks until it was firmly in place. Giving one last nod to his reflection, he turned to head downstairs and lock up the house.

His father had already left for the gala, his mother dashing on his arm in her red gown. Once he met his "date" in front of Lady Anne's, he was sure he'd find them in the grand ballroom at Valeria's main castle.

Striding down the sidewalk, Sebastian clenched his hands at his sides, wondering why he was nervous. It wasn't as if this were a *real* date. Both parties were completing a transaction. He would satisfy society's rules by having someone by his side, and the lady would get gobs of new clothes with the stipend he left at the boutique. A few hours of work with rewards for both.

Then why does tonight feel different?

He had no idea, but perhaps it was the mystery of it all. It wasn't every day he went on a clandestine date with a secret companion. Perhaps he was just reacting to the strange circumstances.

The main square was quiet as most Vampyres were already at the gala. Music wafted from the castle, faint and festive, as Sebastian approached the boutique. Focusing on the figure who slowly came into view, his breath caught in his throat as he studied her.

A long, forest green gown covered a tall body, willowy with slight curves. Long, black hair fell straight down her back, softly flitting in the breeze. Her skin seemed to glow in the moonlight, and his palms suddenly tingled with the urge to touch it...caress it...to see if it was as soft as it appeared.

She turned, facing him fully, and Sebastian felt a jolt in his solar plexus. Her ice-blue eyes shone bright, almost glowing under the stars, and he expelled a breath as he drew closer. Many Vampyres had blue eyes, but hers held the perfect twinge of mischief and innocence. Feeling his body harden, he halted when mere inches separated them.

"Anya?"

White fangs glistened as she smiled under her mask. It was made of elegant black lace and covered her from the tip of her nose to her eyebrows. Black eyelashes extended from those stunning eyes, and his heartbeat escalated as he waited for her to speak.

"You must be Sebastian."

Her voice was husky and slightly hesitant, giving him a small bit of relief. Perhaps he wasn't the only one who'd somehow lost control of his rapid heartbeat. Reaching into his pocket, he pulled out a small corsage.

"It's a poinsettia flower with festive green leaves. I passed a street vendor yesterday who was selling them for the gala and I thought you might like to wear it. If it doesn't clash with your dress," he finished lamely, wondering if he sounded like a dolt. Did men buy women corsages anymore? Hell if he knew. He'd lived for centuries and had no idea what modern dating traditions entailed. When he'd passed the vendor yesterday, he bought it on a whim, wanting to support a small business owner. It also prevented him from showing up empty-handed, but now he was doubting the decision.

"It's lovely," she said, spurring a relieved breath from his chest. "Will you pin it on me? Right here should do." She tapped the collar of her gown, and his eyes trailed to the place where the small swell of her breast rested underneath the silky fabric.

Nodding, he stepped forward, lifting his hand and reclaiming her gaze. "I need to lift the fabric a bit..."

"It's fine," was her raspy reply.

Gently gripping the fabric, he slid the pointed tip of the safety pin through, threading it until he could clasp it. Noticing the slight shake of his hands, he wondered when the hell he'd turned into a nervous schoolboy who couldn't retain his wits. Her skin flushed as he finished clasping the corsage, and he suddenly had images of licking the heated flesh as she pulled him close. Determined to control his reaction, he patted the corsage before stepping back.

"Looks perfect with your dress. You look beautiful, Anya."

One of her gorgeous eyebrows arched. "Even though you can't see my face? Who knows, I could be hideous under here." She pointed to her mask.

Chuckling, he extended his arm. "I don't think so. May I walk you to the gala?"

"Why, of course." She wrapped her arm around his, and they began the three-block walk to the governor's mansion.

"I can't thank you enough for agreeing to this," he said, smiling into her upturned face as they strolled. "I'm a council member and my life is consumed with work. I just don't have time to date."

"I understand. Mila was very clear you aren't interested in any romantic entanglements."

I wasn't...until I saw you standing in the moonlight...

Clearing his throat, he tamped down the inner dialogue. "And what of you? How is it possible none of the bachelors at Astaria snapped you up to be their date?"

"Men are a stubborn lot who only see what they wish to see. I can only assume I wasn't interesting enough to catch anyone's eye."

"Impossible," he breathed, inhaling her scent, which was an intoxicating mixture of roses and evergreen. Sweet and wild, both at once. It suited her perfectly.

Lifting those piercing blue eyes to his, she murmured, "I assure you, Sebastian, it is entirely possible."

He studied her, noticing the white flecks in the blue of her irises...feeling as if he'd stared into them before. As his eyebrows drew together, he asked, "Have we met before? You seem familiar to me."

Something flashed in her eyes, and for a moment he thought it was fear. But it disappeared as quick as lighting, and she straightened her spine. "I rarely leave Astaria, so I doubt it. My parents are aristocrats who decided not to attend tonight because they didn't want the hassle of taking the train to Valeria. Hence why I needed a date. I usually accompany them to formal functions, and didn't want to come solo."

"Well, I'm happy to be of service." He winked and regally circled his hand a few times in front of his waist. "How do you know Mila?"

"I reached out to her several months ago, informing her I would be open to dating but wasn't in the market for a serious relationship yet. Most of her clients are looking for something serious, so it never panned out. Until you," she finished with a cheeky grin.

Thanking the goddess for his fortuity, he vowed not to squander the evening. He had the entire night to talk to her, dance with her...and perhaps even kiss her if the moment felt right. As he gazed at her lips his shaft hardened in his tuxedo pants. He anticipated nibbling them as she moaned in his arms. Her tongue darted out to bathe them, coating the pink flesh with wetness that shone under the street lamps, and he almost groaned. Goddess, he wanted that tongue on his. *Tonight.*

"I'm honored to have you as my date, even if it's only one night and I can't see your face. Or perhaps I can convince you to remove the mask as the night progresses. I *have* been known to be stubbornly persistent. Mila says I'm extremely hardheaded."

Her laughter surrounded them, silky and low, and she shook her head. "The mask stays on. That was the deal."

"I know." He squeezed her wrist. "And I'll also deposit the money at the boutique on Monday. I'm a man of my word."

Her soft grin shot tremors of pleasure through his pulsing body. "I believe you are. Thank you, Sebastian."

They arrived at the mansion, Sebastian walking her up the red-carpeted staircase as the music wafted over them. Once inside, he said obligatory hellos to his friends and fellow council members, introducing Anya as his "friend." Eventually, they made their way to one of the bars in the corner of the ballroom, and he leaned his forearm against it.

"What would you like to drink?"

She perused the bar, gnawing her lip as she pondered. Mesmerized by the action, he didn't hear her when she replied.

"Sebastian?" she called, waving her hand in front of his face.

"Hmm? Sorry. What did you say?"

"Champagne, please."

"Yes, ma'am."

Drawing his wallet from his pocket, he pulled out a stack of liras and gave them to the bartender. "Please keep them coming, and you can keep what's left."

"Sir," the bartender said, counting the bills, "this is seven hundred lira. The drinks are only ten lira each and the proceeds go toward Prince Tordor's human immersion fund."

"I understand. Subtract whatever we have from the total amount and keep the rest as your tip. I already contribute heavily to the immersion fund and want to make sure you and your fellow bartenders are taken care of. You pool tips, right?"

"Yes, sir," he said, excitement lacing his tone. "That's very generous. Thank you." Depositing the money in the cash drawer, he poured Anya's drink before Sebastian ordered a beer.

Once they had their drinks in hand, Sebastian suggested they head to the balcony for some fresh air. Splaying his hand on the small of her back, he led them outside, craving one-on-one time with her so he could get to know her better.

Chapter 5

C eline clenched the glass, her knuckles white with nerves as Sebastian escorted her to the balcony. The heat of his hand sizzled against her back, and she wanted nothing more than to close her eyes and lean into his touch. But they were in public, and he had no idea who she really was, so that fantasy was quickly shooed from her thoughts.

For one moment as they were walking to the gala, he gazed into her eyes and she swore she saw recognition. But alas, he didn't recognize her, and for that, Celine should be grateful.

This is what you wanted, Celine. He's never taken the time to see you. Why do you think he would start now?

"How about here?" he asked, directing them to a secluded spot at the far corner of the sprawling balcony. Resting her forearms on the cool stone, she took a sip of champagne and sighed. "Never can go wrong with fancy champagne on a warm moonlit night, can you?"

"Never," he said, leaning on the balcony beside her. His fingers twirled the glass in his hands as they overlooked the manicured lawn lined with holly bushes planted specifically for the Christmas theme.

"Christmas happens in winter for humans in the Northern hemisphere," he said, "but I do enjoy the warm nights in our realm."

"Me too." Glancing up at him, she reminded herself to ask questions. After all, he was supposed to be a perfect stranger to her. "So, tell me about the council position."

Wrinkling his nose, he considered for a moment before shaking his head. "Usually, I love to talk about my job, but tonight I want to get to know you." His arm scooted closer to hers on the railing, the fabric of his coat brushing against her skin and making it tingle. "Why don't you want a serious relationship? I don't because of my work. What's your excuse?"

Laughing, she shrugged. "Aristocratic women have had the same role for centuries in our king-dom. Queen Miranda and Governor Evie are slowly changing that, but it takes time. I've always been raised to be a proper, refined wife, but honestly, that just sounds so *boring*."

"That it does," he said, chuckling. "If you could do anything, without the restraints of society, what would it be?"

Gazing wistfully at the sky, she released a slow breath. "This probably sounds ridiculous, but I'd like to train children on horses. I was quite fearful of horses when I was young, and we had a fantastic trainer who was extremely patient and helped me get over my fears."

"That doesn't sound ridiculous at all. It's quite noble."

"Not the way my father sees it," she muttered. "I want to teach children everything, not just riding. I think it's important they know how to muck out the stalls, clean the horses, feed them, and everything else. My instructor taught me all those things..."—she traced the balcony as the sad memories surfaced—"until my father realized. He fired the man on the spot because he was teaching me laborer's work. He was only supposed to teach me to ride. The other duties were to be left to the staff."

"Ah, I see." Sebastian's face was contemplative as he sipped his beer. "Old traditions of the Vampyre kingdom are deeply embedded, especially in the older generations. Your father probably thought he was protecting your aristocratic nature or some such nonsense."

Her eyes widened as she studied him. "You wouldn't have a problem with an aristocratic woman doing laborer's work...and making a living from it?"

Pursing his lips, he pondered. "I don't think so if it made her happy. Hell, Anya, our lives are long. If we're not doing want makes us happy, what's the damn point?"

Smiling, she lifted her glass. "Exactly."

Clinking their glasses, they gazed into each other's eyes as they drank.

Sebastian's eyes smoldered behind his white mask, causing her breath to hitch. Ever so slowly, he reached over and brushed the skin of her shoulder.

"A piece of pollen," he said softly, his fingers swiping her skin in a soft caress. "All gone."

His touch lingered as if he didn't want to pull away, and she felt the thrumming of her heartbeat in her throat. Struggling to breathe, she gazed into his deep brown eyes, wondering if she'd ever been in such close proximity to him. His musky scent filled her nostrils, and she fought the urge to close her eyes and savor it. Feeling her throat bob, she searched for something to say to break the heavy silence.

"My dear Anya," he said, lowering his hand and giving a formal bow. "I fear I cannot go another moment without dancing with you." Extending his hand, his fangs glowed atop his lower lip as he smiled. "Will you please do me the honor?"

Setting her glass on the ledge, she took his hand, nodding since her throat was too dry to speak. Sebastian had finally asked her to dance after all these years. Well, he'd asked *Anya*, but still, it was extremely special to her.

Knowing she would cherish every moment his body was pressed to hers on the dance floor, she followed him inside, her steps echoing in tandem with her rapid heartbeat.

S ebastian led Anya to the dance floor, hoping she didn't notice the slight sheen of sweat on his palm. Her proximity was like a tuning fork; the closer she got, the more every cell in his frame seemed to vibrate. Leading her to the dance floor, he slid one arm around her waist and held up his other one.

"Is this okay?"

She nodded, the lower half of her cheeks flushing as she took his hand. Gently gripping her waist, he began to move. Forward...back...in the rhythm of the formal dance steps he'd learned as a child, while the band played in the background.

Anya matched him step for step, and he was impressed with her skills. "You're an excellent dancer."

"A must for a proper aristocratic Vampyre female, no?" She cocked a brow as they swayed.

"Absolutely. Still, I think I'd rather see how you fare mucking a stall. For some reason, I can't imagine it."

Tossing her head back, she laughed, exposing the line of her throat. Sebastian's fangs itched to touch her there...to scrape the delicate skin as she clutched his shoulders, begging for more...

"Well, my father owns our stables and I'm on strict orders not to go inside. The horse must be prepared for me by the staff so I can ride it without getting dirty." Sighing, her lips formed a slight pout. "It's so fun to get dirty though."

"I think I'd like to get dirty with you," he murmured before he could stop the silken words.

Her hand tightened as her lips fell open, slightly stunned. But Sebastian also saw the burning desire in her eyes, and a thrill shot down his spine that she felt their attraction too.

"Did I shock you, darling?" he asked, drawing her closer as their bodies moved in tandem. "I would apologize, but I think you liked it."

A stuttered breath left her lungs before she formed a slight grin. "I *did* like it," she whispered. "For someone who doesn't want a relationship, you certainly are a flirt."

"Only with women who will disappear at midnight, leaving me heartbroken and alone," he teased. "So, I need to take advantage of our time together."

Leaning into him, she rested her cheek on his chest, withdrawing her hand from his and sliding it around his neck. "I would like that," she murmured, pressing her body closer to his. "You can take advantage of me until midnight, Sebastian."

Gliding his arm around her waist, he spread both palms over her back, caressing it through the silken fabric of her dress. Pressing his cheek against her hair, he melded their bodies, marveling at how well they fit. Her lithe frame and subtle curves pushed against his firm muscles, and he almost sighed in contentment.

As they danced and he inhaled her fragrant skin, another aroma wafted toward his nostrils. Clenching his teeth, a muscle flexed in his jaw as he smelled her arousal. Vampyres had highly evolved senses, and males could inherently smell a female's arousal. It was extremely intoxicating, and his body jumped into action, ready to mate. His cock sprang to life inside his pants, and his heart hammered in his chest as he wondered if she would push him away.

He knew the moment she felt his rapidly swelling cock push against her lower abdomen. Inhaling a quick breath, her fingers tightened on the back of his neck.

"I'm sorry," he whispered, half-embarrassed and half-joyful she knew he was aroused. Sebastian was an extremely forthright man, and he had no desire to hide his attraction. Hell, he wanted nothing more than to kiss her before the night was over, so she might as well know he was viscerally attracted to her.

"Do you want to stop dancing?"

She shook her head against his chest, and his eyes narrowed at the feel of her hair along his jaw. For some reason, it felt coarser than he'd imagined. More synthetic in a way. Still, he reveled in having her pressed against him and felt the tension leave his muscles when he spoke.

"You must smell my arousal," she said softly. The skin of her neck turned a deep red, and he chuckled at her embarrassment.

"Thank the goddess the lights are dim and we're on the corner of the dance floor. Our bodies seem to have a mind of their own, although I'm not complaining."

"Me neither." Her arms tightened around his neck, and he took the cue, tugging her so close their bodies seemed to morph together. His erection stood proud against her stomach as her desire-laced scent surrounded them, and Sebastian held tight, wishing the night would never end.

Eventually, the band took a break and the lights were raised so Sofia could address the room. After completing the very difficult task of letting Anya go, he led her to stand with the other immortals so they could hear the speech.

"Thank you all so much for coming to our Christmas gala," Sofia said, lifting her wineglass to the gala attendees. "Christmas is a very special time for human Christians like me. I know you all worship Etherya, and I'm honored she gave her blessing to throw this fete."

"Plus, it allows me to show off my DJ skills," Heden said, throwing his arm around Sofia's shoulders and lifting his beer. "I have the coolest playlist. You all are going to love it—"

"Not happening!" Miranda's voice chimed from the back of the room.

"Jeez, Miranda, let a brother live a little," Heden said as the crowd chuckled. "I know you secretly love my playlists. I made one specifically for you and my brother to knock boots so you could have a new heir, and look how that turned out."

"You're *not* getting credit for this," Miranda said, rubbing her extended belly as Sathan's thick arm surrounded her, his expression morose at his brother's antics. "Although I think Sathan *did* develop an unhealthy obsession with human pop music thanks to your playlist."

"If I have to listen to Lizzo one more time, I'll burst my own damn eardrums," Sathan droned, squeezing Miranda's shoulder. "You created a monster."

"Okay, okay, *I'm* the one who likes pop music. Who knew? Lizzo's pretty badass, and it's catchy."

She grinned at Sathan and scrunched her features. "Anyway, carry on, Sofia."

Laughing, Sofia continued. "To close, I'd like to remind you we have several stations you can swing by to learn more about our culture. I'm running one, and Evie and Arderin are too since they lived in the human world and have experience there."

Both women waved, flashing welcoming grins as they stood beside Miranda and Sathan.

"And now, I urge you to have fun and remember, if you walk underneath mistletoe, you have to kiss the person closest to you. Enjoy!"

The crowd gave a raucous cheer before dispersing, many heading to the various stations to learn about the Christmas story, the three wise men, Santa Claus, and more.

Turning to Anya, Sebastian asked, "Do you want to visit any of the stations?"

Biting her lip, a hint of mischief flared in her eyes. "I know we should, but is it terrible that I don't want to? We only have two hours before I walk back to the train, and I was having so much fun dancing. Maybe we can have another drink on the balcony and wait for the band to start again..."

"I'd love that." Extending his hand, he gestured for her to lead. "After you, darling."

She shivered slightly at the endearment, causing Sebastian's heart to *thunk* in his chest. Determined to whisper the tender word in her ear before the night was over, he followed her to the bar, enamored by the gentle sway of her hips in the stunning gown.

Chapter 6

After another round of playful and intimate conversation, Celine danced with Sebastian until the band played their last song. As the lights lifted and people began to exit the ballroom, she lifted sad eyes to her handsome date.

"Well, I guess that's our cue to leave. I was having so much fun."

"Me too." Hesitation lined his expression as he held out his hand. "Can I at least walk you to the train? I promise I'll be a perfect gentleman."

Nodding, she placed her hand in his, and they exited the mansion to the sidewalk. Setting a leisurely pace, Celine placed her arm in the crook of his, hoping to draw out her time with him as much as possible. How could she ever go back to real life where he ignored her? A small part of her wanted to rip off the wig and mask, grab his arms, and shake him.

"*Look at me*," she would plead as he finally understood it was *her*, the woman he'd been intent on ignoring for centuries.

But that was a fantasy for a woman more confident than Celine. Although she was proud of herself for her courage this evening, it only went so far. After years of rejection, she just didn't dare to take a chance. If he rejected her, she might not survive the emotional fallout.

So, she walked with him to the train, reveling in how charming he was as they chatted. When they arrived at the underground platform, she turned to face him, feeling nervous. Crossing her arms over her chest, she rubbed them, wondering if he would try to kiss her.

"I had a lovely time," he said.

"Me too. Thank you, Sebastian."

"Come, let's have a bit of privacy." After leading them to a secluded spot under some nearby trees, he reached into his jacket pocket. Pulling out a bundle of mistletoe, he flashed a grin as he held it over her head. "Would I be extremely cheesy if I stole this from the party so I'd have an excuse to kiss you?"

Breathing a laugh, she stepped closer, threading her arms around his neck. "You don't need an excuse, but it's very cute." Rising to her toes, she whispered, "Please kiss me, Sebastian."

His arm snaked around her waist as he tossed the mistletoe aside. Drawing her into his warm body, he slid his hand to her nape, supporting her as his fingers slid over the cap of the wig.

"Oh, I...uh...just got my hair done, so my scalp is very tender. Probably better to hold my neck."

A strange look crossed his expression before he nodded, sliding his hand down and cupping her neck. "Like this?" he murmured, moving closer.

"Like that," she sighed, thankful he hadn't realized she was wearing a wig.

Grazing her lips with his, he gently pushed them open before sliding his tongue over her top lip...and then her bottom one...

Celine groaned, her eyes closing as elation coursed through her frame. Spearing her fingernails into his neck, she urged him closer, her body shuddering at his low growl.

His tongue speared into her mouth, licking...tasting...as she tentatively touched her tongue to his.

"Yes, darling..." he rasped, sucking her tongue between his full lips...drawing her further into the kiss. "Use that sexy little tongue and kiss me back. Show me you want me half as much as I want you."

Whimpering with desire, she slid her tongue in one slow stroke over his, a small laugh escaping her throat when he cursed.

"Damn, woman," he groaned, nipping her lip with his fangs. "You're going to kill me. Do that again."

Feeling her confidence soar, she began to kiss him in earnest, sliding her tongue over his, moving her lips in tandem with his thick ones as he pressed his erection into her stomach. His tongue mated with hers, darting over every crevice of her mouth before he drew back and trailed a line of kisses over her cheek to her ear. Resting his mouth against the shell of her ear, he whispered, "Take off the mask, Anya."

"Noooo..." she moaned, her knees buckling when he licked the sensitive shell of her ear before gently biting the lobe.

"Please, sweetheart. This can't be the end. I need to see you again."

"I can't," she said, placing her palms on his chest but unable to push him away. "Only one night. We had a deal."

Lifting his head, his deep brown eyes searched hers, filled with lust and blazing regret. "I never should've agreed to one night. I didn't think this would happen."

Needing to break contact, she turned, resting her head in her hand. "Sebastian, I...oh goddess, this is a mess..."

His fingers trailed over the back of her neck as he brushed the long hair of the wig aside, placing it to lie over her shoulder. Replacing his fingers with his lips, he trailed soft kisses over the swell of her shoulder while her body shook with desire.

"You have a birthmark here," he murmured against her skin. A moment later, she felt his wet tongue glide over the mark above her shoulder blade. "I'd love to see your other ones, Anya. Perhaps you have one on your leg too." His hand trailed over her thigh toward the slit in her dress. "Or on your inner thigh..."

Wanting to sob in frustration, she halted his hand before it could slip under her dress. "I'm sorry," she whispered, wishing she'd never come up with the stupid scheme. Now that she'd kissed him, it would be impossible to stop pining for him. Furthermore, he was now infatuated with a woman who didn't exist. Cursing herself, she turned and placed her palms on his pecs.

"I had a lovely time, but I have to go. Thank you, Sebastian. I wish you all the best. Good night."

Turning, she tried to flee, but he grabbed her wrist, halting her. "Please, Anya, if you just give me a chance—"

A frustrated huff left her lips as she clenched her fist. "A chance? A chance?" Telling herself not to blow it, she tamped down the exasperated scream lodged in the back of her throat. "You're a fool, Sebastian, but I'm no better. This was a mistake. Good night." Dislodging her wrist from his grasp, she turned and ran to the platform, disappearing down the stairs to the underground station as he called her name.

Called *Anya's* name.

Not wanting him to follow her, she ran to the bathroom, knowing someone as polite as Sebastian would never follow her inside. And then she waited...for what seemed like hours, but it was only minutes in the scheme of things.

Stepping toward the long mirror above the sinks, she took off her mask and wig, massaging her scalp as she set her blond hair free. Staring deep into her own eyes, her chin trembled as she realized she was doomed. Never would she forget the taste of Sebastian on her lips...or her tongue...or *in her mouth*...

Touching her lips, she licked them, savoring the taste of the man she'd loved since she knew what the word meant. Then she picked up her wig and mask and left the station. Her walk home was brisk since she wanted nothing more than to curl up in her bed and cry.

Once she got home, she snuck through the back door and tiptoed up the stairs. After washing her face and brushing her teeth, she slid into bed, knowing her family believed she'd been there all night.

"You never should've lied to them, Celine," she said, punching the pillow. "You never should've lied to *him*. Oh goddess, what have I done?"

Clutching the pillow close, she buried her face in the soft feathers and cried herself to sleep.

Chapter 7

Sebastian walked home from the train in a daze, confused by how things had gone so horribly wrong. One minute, he was involved in the most erotic kiss of his life. The next, Anya was pulling away and running to the station. After he'd recovered from the shock, he jogged down the stairs to find her. She'd all but disappeared, and he certainly didn't want to make the situation worse by seeking out a woman who was vehemently trying to flee, so he'd trudged up the platform stairs and headed home.

Once back in his father's opulent mansion, he slid into bed and settled in the darkness. Wondering how it had all gone wrong, he slid his hands under his head on the pillow as the ceiling fan whirled above.

"You should've never asked her to remove the mask, Sebastian," he muttered, furious with himself. "It was the one stipulation you agreed to, and you blew it." Rolling over, he punched the pillow, knowing he would get no rest as thoughts of Anya flitted through his mind.

On Monday, Sebastian walked to work, noting the streets had been cleared of the Christmas decorations. They were disassembled and put away, vanished as effectively as his sultry night with Anya. Scoffing, a part of him wondered if it had all been a dream.

During lunch, he strolled to the boutique and opened a private account in Anya's name.

"Do you have her father's name, sir?"

"No," he mused as his eyebrows drew together. Citizens in the immortal world didn't use last names. Instead, they were referred to by their father's name. He was Sebastian, son of Astaroth. And Anya was the daughter of...well, he had no idea since he'd agreed to her anonymity.

"When she comes in to claim it, ask her what it's for. She'll mention the Christmas gala. I think that will be enough to identify her."

"Will do, sir," the owner said. "This is a nice stipend, and I appreciate your business."

Always happy to support a local business owner, he gave her a brisk nod before leaving.

Instead of heading back to his office, Sebastian trailed through town, ending up at Mila's office. Hell, he didn't even know his legs were carrying him there until his hand was on the doorknob. Turning it, he stepped inside as the bell rang above his head.

"Well, look what the cat dragged in," she said, threading her hands behind her head as she sat at the desk in the small office. "You look like crap."

"I can always count on you to bring my ego down a few notches," he muttered, lowering into the chair in front of her desk. Resting his palms on the smooth surface, he lightly gripped the wood. "I need to know how to contact her, Mila. Please."

"Wow," she breathed, leaning back in her chair and crossing her ankles atop her desk. "I can't believe it. You're interested in a woman. I'd almost given up hope."

"I don't know what it was about her." He circled his hand, leaning back in the chair and resting his forehead on his fingers. "Maybe it was the mystery of it all. I've never felt attraction like this. It was just...*easy* with her, you know?"

Mila squinted one eye as she bit the inside of her cheek. "I think you're right. The anonymity and lack of commitment allowed you to relax and be open. And once you were open, your attraction and intuition took over."

"Maybe," he said, rubbing his forehead. "I did feel relaxed with her. Bachelors in our kingdom are always on guard because meddling parents are trying to make bonding matches. Since that wasn't a possibility with her, I felt free."

"I'm glad to hear that, Sebastian, honestly, but I can't give you her identity. You know that."

Frustrated, he picked at a stray thread on the side of his dress pants. "I don't want you to break your word. It's just..." Lifting his gaze to hers, he tamped down the urge to plead for Anya's phone number...or her address...or anything that would allow him to locate her. "I think she might be my mate."

Arching her brows, Mila dropped her legs to the floor. Leaning forward, she rested her forearms on the table. "Sebastian, nothing would make me happier."

"But if I can't locate her—"

"You'll figure it out," she interrupted, holding up a finger. "You're a stubborn son of a bitch if I've ever met one, and if she's truly your mate, you'll find a way."

Sighing, he nodded, frustrated when her office phone rang.

"I hate to kick you out, but Mondays are busy here. Everyone who had a terrible date over the weekend wants to start fresh."

Standing, he ran his hand through his hair. "I'm going to find her, Mila. Mark my words."

As she reached for the phone he noticed the mischievous glint in her eyes. "I'm counting down the days until you do." Lifting the receiver to her ear, she shooed him away.

Determination welled in his gut as he exited her office and strode through the main square. Failure was not an option, and Sebastian would stop at nothing to find his mystery woman.

Chapter 8

C eline's phone rang promptly at 7 p.m. Monday evening. After her epic crying session on Saturday night, she'd woken up the next morning with a sense of firm resolve. She had made the decision to deceive Sebastian, and although she felt terrible about it, it had led to the only kiss she would probably ever share with him.

And oh, how magnificent the kiss had been. Celine had only been kissed by a handful of men in the past, and none of them came close to Sebastian's skillful ministrations upon her lips. Knowing she would treasure his taste and sultry words for years to come, she rose and reminded herself to buck up. She was a strong woman—stronger than many gave her credit for—and she needed to start living that way.

"Did I lose you?" Mila asked on the other end of the line.

"No," Celine said, putting the phone on speaker as she washed her hands. "I just came in from the stables."

Silence stretched as her friend contemplated. "Umm, I thought Handor forbade you from going inside the stables. Aren't your fancy servants supposed to do all the dirty work for you?"

"They're my father's staff, not servants, and I'm tired of not pulling my weight in my own damn life. I love horses and told the foreman I want full access to the stables."

"That's probably going to get him fired," she said acerbically.

"I won't let that happen. Anyway, what's up? I need to get ready for dinner with the family in a few minutes."

"Sebastian came to my office today. He wants to see Anya again."

Celine's heart nearly leaped from her chest. "What did you tell him?"

"That I wouldn't do it. But he's got that determined glint in his eyes, Celine. He's stubborn, so I'm not sure what's going to happen. Oh, and he left the stipend at the boutique in Anya's name."

Frowning, Celine decided to donate it as quickly as possible. Something about having a financial "transaction" between them didn't sit right in her gut. "I'll stop by tomorrow and give instructions on where to donate it. I bet it will buy nice gowns for several girls at Lynia and Naria who need dresses for their formal school dances."

"That's very generous, Celine."

"It's what any decent person would do."

"Well, that's the problem, honey," Mila said, breathing a soft laugh. "Some people just aren't decent. Okay, I've got to run, but I just wanted you to know Sebastian's sniffing around. Honestly, I hope he figures it out. I think he needs to know the woman who set his world on fire Saturday night was *you*."

"He'll never believe it," she said, her tone sad as she traced the porcelain. "He doesn't see me that way—"

"Then *make* him see you that way, Celine. Show him who you really are."

Sighing, she digested the words.

"Okay, gotta go. Bye."

The screen went dark, and Celine mulled over her friend's words. Gripping the edge of the sink, she stared at her reflection, allowing herself to feel her inner strength. She'd expressed it today when she told the foreman to give her full access to the stables. Could she go further and express it around Sebastian? For some reason, the thought was terrifying.

Deciding to shelve it so she could prepare for dinner, Celine eventually headed downstairs, distracted as she met her brothers for a pre-dinner drink in the den.

As the week progressed, Sebastian found himself walking past the boutique quite often. Although he told himself he needed fresh air and exercise, the truth was that he was hoping to catch a glimpse of Anya entering the store. If he could catch her when she went to claim the stipend he'd deposited, he could at least *try* to get her to agree to see him again.

As he strolled past the boutique after finishing his morning paperwork, he glanced through the window and noticed Celine settling up at the register. She was having an animate conversation with the boutique owner, who eventually bounded around the counter and enveloped Celine in a firm hug. Curious, Sebastian waited until they were finished, grinning at Celine as she exited the store.

"Oh," she said, pulling the door shut. "Hello, Sebastian." She pasted on a grin, although it didn't reach her eyes. "Fancy seeing you here in the middle of the workday."

"It's a nice day for a stroll, and I've realized recently I don't take enough breaks during the day." His eyes darted to the boutique owner through the window before returning to hers. "You two seemed to be embroiled in an exciting discussion."

"Oh,"—she waved her hand flippantly—"that was nothing. I was just checking on an order I placed for some gowns. I'm one of her frequent customers, so she dotes on me."

"Hmm..." was his soft reply as he studied her. Sebastian had known Celine forever, although he'd rarely made the time to speak to her alone. Why bother when she was born to be someone's aristocratic bonded mate and he had no desire to bond with anyone? Furthermore, his father had concocted some hair-brained scheme to set Celine up with Garridan, although it had backfired when he fell for Siora.

Studying the woman in front of him, Sebastian took a moment to actually *see* her. Yes, she was known as one of the most beautiful women on the compound, but had he ever really looked at her? Although she had blond hair, her eyelashes were long and dark. They extended above her ice-blue eyes, bracketing them so they shone in the sunlight.

As the silence deepened, her pale cheeks inflamed, the reddish flush extending down her neck as the pulse there thrummed. A small wisp of something sweet and airy entered his nostrils, and he inhaled, savoring the scent. It was one of roses and evergreen, so similar to Anya's...

"Well, I have to meet my brother at the coffee shop," she said, clearing her throat as she backed away. "It was lovely to see you, Sebastian."

Pivoting, she rushed across the street while he stood frozen on the sidewalk. Had Celine always had such an intoxicating scent? And why in the goddess's name was it so similar to Anya's? Deciding he was promptly losing his mind due to a longing for a woman he might never see again, he shook off the encounter and continued down the street.

By the next day, the curiosity was too much to bear, so Sebastian entered the boutique to ask the owner if his stipend had been claimed.

"Oh! Yes, sir," she said, excited as she held up some silky fabric behind the counter. "Your lovely recipient donated the entire amount to two girls' schools at Lynia and Naria. It will allow me to make thirty beautiful gowns for girls who couldn't afford them otherwise. May the goddess bless you both."

"That's quite generous," he said, taken by the gesture. "Did she request to leave me a message or note, perhaps?"

"Oh, I'm sorry, sir, but she requested to remain anonymous. She did say she had a splendid evening with you. She's such a lovely girl, our Cel—" Covering her lips with her fingers, the shop owner gasped. "Our *celebrated* donor."

Sebastian's eyes narrowed as he wondered if the woman was hiding something. "Yes, she is quite special. Thank you, ma'am. Take care."

Exiting the store, Sebastian strolled down the cobblestone sidewalk, wondering when his life had become a strange amalgamation of coded conversations and unrequited attraction. No wonder he'd never thrown his hat in the dating ring. The entire situation was quite maddening.

By Friday, after several sweat-soaked, sleepless nights dreaming of Anya, Sebastian decided he might not be cut out for romance of any kind. His thoughts were consumed with his mystery woman, and worse, last night he'd dreamed of Celine.

Sweet, quiet, biddable Celine.

It made absolutely no sense.

As he'd thrashed in bed, visions of Anya had plagued him: her gorgeous eyes and full lips, glistening under the moonlight as they stood in the secluded park by the train. But then her eyes had widened, those glorious eyelashes lifting as she removed her mask. Celine's face remained, her scent the same as Anya's...roses and evergreen...and he reached for her as she backed away, tears streaming down her cheeks as she cursed him for not knowing what was real...

He'd awoken with a gasp, struggling to breathe. After chugging some ice-cold water, he'd returned to bed, his thoughts consumed with the unmistakable knowledge his mystery woman and Celine shared the same addictive aroma.

When he finally did make it to work, he was distracted and could barely complete any of the projects on his desk. Deciding to take a walk, he strolled toward the main square, his heart leaping in his throat as Celine and her brother approached.

"Good morning, Xandor," he called, nodding before resting his gaze on his companion. "Celine," he softly murmured.

Her throat bobbed under the pale skin of her neck, sending a jolt of awareness to his shaft. Had her skin always been so creamy and smooth? What would it feel like to graze his fangs over it? To make her moan before he plunged them deep inside her pulsing vein...

Briefly closing his eyes, he wondered what the hell was happening to him. He'd gone from fantasizing about a phantom lover to fantasizing about Celine of all people. Someone he'd convinced himself he could never be interested in...

"Hello, Sebastian." The slight gravel in her voice seemed to wrap around his skin, caressing it like a feather that fell from the sky. As his heartbeat accelerated in his chest, he continued the conversation, attempting to maintain appearances.

"I hear you're going to be joining me on the council soon. Your father is excited to retire and proud to have you take his place."

"I'm ready to fulfill my duty," Xander said with a broad smile. "And perhaps it will help my little sister here finally find a mate. She will now be related to *two* council members, one former and one current."

"Thank you, but I've done just fine without a mate so far," she said, swiping his arm off her shoulders. "And I don't need you or father to matchmake for me."

"Ah, our feisty sister. Many think she's timid because society taught her to act that way, but you should see her at home, Sebastian. Why, just yesterday I caught her washing one of our horses in the stable. Can you imagine? We have a staff of fifty, but she insists on doing laborers' work. It baffles the mind."

"The horse's name is Lucy, and she gave me a magnificent ride through the meadow," Celine said, crossing her arms. "I only felt it proper to give her a warm bath afterward."

Sebastian's gaze flickered to hers, covered with indignation as she scowled at her brother. A memory of the conversation he'd had with Anya about her wanting to work with horses flitted through his mind. Information slowly began to click together as his wheels churned like puzzle pieces that had finally found their match, solving the mystery he'd somehow already unconsciously known.

"Our altruistic sister," Xandor continued. "Why, the other day, I overheard her talking to Mila about a large donation she made to purchase gowns for girls on Lynia and Naria. First horse baths, and now this—"

Covering her brother's mouth with her hand, Celine hissed, "Will you shut up? You shouldn't eavesdrop on private conversations."

Chuckling, he removed her hand. "As I said,"—he cocked an eyebrow at Sebastian—"feisty as hell, although no one outside of our home truly knows. Such a shame."

"Oh, you're infuriating," she cried, stomping her foot. "I'm going to see Mila. You can have coffee alone since you're intent on mocking me."

Huffing, she pivoted and began walking down the street toward Mila's office.

"Celine," Xandor called, amusement in his voice. "Come now, don't storm away!"

She held up a hand, waving him off, and Sebastian thought she'd most likely flip him off if she weren't so proper.

"She's been crabby all week, ever since she was ill and couldn't attend the Christmas gala. Women," he muttered, rubbing his forehead, "am I right?"

Sebastian could only nod as the breadth of information rushed through him. Celine's scent was eerily similar to Anya's. She enjoyed bathing her horse in the stables too. She'd recently made a donation from the boutique. She didn't attend the gala on Saturday...

He hadn't even noticed she wasn't in attendance, but that was par for the course with Celine. He rarely noticed anything about her...until recently...until she'd *forced* him to...

Overwhelmed with the stunning conclusion his brain was quickly drawing, Sebastian struggled to catch his breath as the unshakable truth assuaged him: Anya *was* Celine.

"Are you okay, Sebastian?" Xandor asked, cupping his shoulder. "You look quite pale."

"I'm fine," he said, backing away and showing his palms. "Just a flush of heat from the sun. I have to get back to work, Xandor. Excited to work with you on the council. Take care."

Turning, he strode to the nearest park, seeking solace. Resting his palm on the firm bark of a tree, he inhaled several deep breaths, disbelief coursing through his frame.

"Why would she deceive me?" he asked, the words quiet and filled with equal parts anger and incredulity.

The chirping birds held no answer as he clenched his fingers on the bark. Desperate for answers, he did his best to quell the rage as he pushed away from the tree, striding from the park toward Mila's office, knowing Celine would be there.

After a week of sleepless nights and unsated desire, it was time for Sebastian to get some answers.

Chapter 9

C eline rushed inside Mila's office, closing the door behind her and sprinting to her desk. Placing her palms on the wood, she cried, "He knows, Mila! Oh goddess, he knows." Sinking into the nearby chair, she buried her face in her hands and tried to hold back the tears.

"Okay, okay," Mila said, grabbing a tissue and striding over to sit beside her. "This isn't the end of the world, Celine. After all, you had to know he'd eventually find out. Perhaps a small piece of you wanted that, hmm?"

Sniffling, Celine took the tissue and swiped her nose. "I didn't want him to hate me. At least in the past he was just indifferent toward me. Now that I've deceived him he's going to detest me, Mila."

"Don't jump to conclusions," she said, rubbing her shoulder. "He was pretty torn up about you when I saw him earlier this week—"

"That was about *Anya*, not me—"

"*You* are Anya, Celine. You told me you felt confident when you were able to be someone else, but it was always *you* inside. You need to be strong and show him you're the one he wanted the whole time."

"Oh goddess, this is a mess." Tossing the tissue into the wastebasket, she wiped her cheeks. "I should've just left him alone."

Arching her eyebrow, a knowing glint entered Mila's eyes. "I'm glad you didn't. I think it's finally time you ruffled his feathers."

Several loud knocks pounded on the door, causing them both to gasp.

Patting Celine's shoulder, Mila leaned down and whispered, "Give him hell." Stalking to the door, she pulled it open and said, "Where's the fire? I heard you the first time you knocked."

Sebastian breezed past her, fire in his eyes as he gazed at Celine. When he lifted his finger she noticed it shook with rage. "What the hell, Celine?" he asked, nostrils flaring as he stared her down. "I want answers!"

"Whew, he's pissed," Mila said, her eyes widening as she spared Celine a mocking grimace. "I'm out. Don't break anything in my office. I'll be back in an hour. Ta-ta!" With a breezy wave, she darted from the office, closing the door firmly behind her.

Sebastian focused on Celine, anger oozing from his large frame as he slowly approached. Rising, she backed away until her backside hit the desk. Unable to escape, she gripped the edge of the wood, wondering if she'd ever seen such emotion in his usually stoic expression.

Reaching her, he leaned forward, bracketing her with his arms as his palms rested on the desk. Small pants left her lungs as her body ached to press against his while simultaneously knowing she needed to retreat. Staring deep into his brown eyes, she waited, trapped as effectively as the rabbits her father snared for hunting.

"I thought I was going mad," he gritted, his face so close she could feel his warm breath on her cheek. "Every time I saw you...or *smelled* you...I thought of *her*..."

"I'm sorry," she whispered, shaking her head.

"And every time I dreamed of her, I began to dream of *you*..."

Lifting his hand, he touched his finger to her cheek. Inhaling a swift breath, she waited, wondering if he would strike her. His cheeks were flushed with anger, and rage simmered in his eyes. But she also saw a slight bit of arousal in the brown depths, jump-starting her body's reaction as she absorbed his nearness.

"Oh, no," he said, shaking his head, "I'm not going to strike you. Any man who does that isn't worth his mettle." Gliding his finger across her cheek, he caressed the corner of her mouth before slowly dragging his finger across her bottom lip. Desire surged to her core, and she felt a resulting rush of wetness as she grew slick between her thighs.

Closing his eyes, he inhaled, savoring the aroma of her arousal before lifting his lids. Softly caressing her lip, his fangs glistened as heavy breaths exited his lungs.

"I thought I'd never smell this arousal again...but here it is, smothering me in the most pleasurable way." Dipping his finger inside her mouth, he touched the wetness, setting her body on fire.

A whimper leaped from her throat as he softly moaned.

"Damn it, Celine," he whispered, rimming her mouth with his finger. "I don't understand any of this. All I know is that I'm furious...and that I want you so badly I fear I might explode if I don't kiss you..."

Desperate to show him she was sorry for her deception, she closed her mouth around his finger, drawing him inside as he groaned. Gazing into his eyes, she sucked him, gliding her tongue over his skin as he emitted a low growl.

"Goddess, Celine," he rasped, inching closer as he moved his finger between her lips. "Where have you been hiding all this time?"

She gently bit his finger, causing a rush of air to escape his lungs before he withdrew it.

"I've always been in front of you, but you've never seen me, Sebastian. *Never*—"

Pressing his body to hers, he touched his lips to her trembling ones, cutting off her words and stealing her breath.

"So you deceived me? Made me look like a fool?"

"I never wanted that," she rasped, drowning in his musky scent and the heat of his body. "I just wanted you to *see* me—"

His hand shot to her nape, threading through her thick hair and tugging so she was forced to tilt her head back. Caught in his grasp, she waited.

"Damn you," he murmured against her lips. "I can't decide whether I want to strangle you or fuck you, Celine—"

Unable to control her desperate need to taste him, she speared her tongue into his mouth. Sliding her arms around his neck, she perched on the desk, lifting her legs to wrap them around his waist. Strong fingers tightened in her hair as he pulled her against his body, his other arm snaking around her waist to hold her close. Moaning her name, he began to kiss her in earnest, his talented tongue gliding over hers as she responded with ardor.

He tasted every crevice of her mouth, working furiously as his body grew even harder with arousal. Reveling in the feel of his erection between her legs, she pushed her mound against it, a fresh rush of slick coating her core when he groaned.

"Look at you pushing into my cock, Celine," he murmured, his tongue circling her lips as he dropped his hand from her waist to her thigh. His large palm slid over the silken fabric of her dress, inching ever so close to the slit that ran down the left side. "Do you want to feel it against you when there's nothing between us? What have you been hiding under all these formal dresses? Are you wet for me, sweetheart?"

Unable to control the undulation of her hips, she closed her eyes, pushing toward him as a stuttered breath left her lungs. In truth, she hated the formal gowns of the Vampyre aristocracy but usually wore them in public to please her father since he was deeply concerned with appearances.

"So greedy," he hummed, gliding his fingers past the slit to her inner thigh. Goose bumps appeared under his skillful hand as he caressed a trail to her mound. Resting his forehead against hers, he softly commanded, "Look at me."

Fear that he would laugh at her—or worse, reject her—coursed through her frame, but she pushed it aside and lifted her lids. Brown orbs glazed with lust stared back at her as he traced his finger over her wet thong.

"Such naughty panties for such a proper woman," he rasped, trailing his finger up and down the wet fabric. "You have everyone fooled, don't you, Celine?"

"I only want to be myself," she whispered, shaking her head. "Everyone else decided who I was before I got the chance."

"Such a waste," he murmured, sweeping the thin fabric aside to trace the lips of her core. "You've been hiding this sweet, slick treasure from me for ages, haven't you?"

Whimpering, she nodded. "I've wanted you like this for so long..."

"Like this?" he asked, rimming her opening with his finger. Saliva pooled in her mouth at the intimate gesture as he began to push inside. "Or, like this?" Gently probing, he nudged into her wet channel, a ragged moan escaping his lips as he pushed deeper...

"Like that," she whispered.

"Dirty girl," he murmured, nipping her lips. "Has anyone ever touched you here, Celine?"

"No..." Threading her fingers in his hair, she held tight, embarrassment swamping her at her lack of experience. "No one ever wanted to touch me there..."

"Fools," he rasped, slowly moving his finger in and out of her tight vise. "Every man on this damn compound is a fool, and I'm the biggest one of all." Drawing her into a kiss, his tongue played with hers as he impaled her with his finger. "Spread your legs wider," he softly commanded into her mouth.

She complied, elated at the pleasure that reverberated through his frame at her acquiescence. Drawing her bottom lip between his teeth, he gently sucked her as he inserted two fingers into her quivering body.

"Good girl," he murmured, pressing soft kisses to her lips as his fingers moved within. "Do you like that, Celine?"

"Yes...."

Gathering her wetness on his fingers, he trailed up her folds, burrowing under the hood of her mound to the spot filled with a thousand nerve-endings. "Have you ever had an orgasm?"

She nodded, unable to speak with his fingers against her deepest place.

"Who gave you the orgasm?" he growled, possession lacing his tone.

"Me. I'm the only one who's ever touched myself there...until now..."

"Thank the goddess," he whispered against her lips. "I thought I was going to have to murder someone."

A shocked giggle escaped her lips as she reveled in the possessive words. "I only ever wanted you to touch me there, Sebastian...*oh god*..."

His fingers made concentric circles over her swollen little bud, generating such pleasure she thought she might melt into a pool of lust in his arms. Digging her fingernails into his shoulders, she searched for a stronghold as he took her higher.

"First, you're going to come in my arms, Celine. Do you hear me?"

"Yes," she cried, her mouth falling open as he spoke the dirty words.

"Then you're going to tell me why you deceived me."

The pressure of his fingers increased, causing stars to appear behind her closed lids as she neared the peak.

Pressing his lips to her ear, he tenderly licked the lobe before nipping it with his fangs. "Come for me, naughty girl. Come, and I just might forgive you..."

"Oh...I...*Sebastian!*" Tossing her head back, Celine clutched his broad shoulders, squeezing with all her might as she dove headfirst into the most spectacular orgasm of her life. Losing control, her body quaked and shuddered as Sebastian whispered words of praise in her ear. Cupping her mound, he held tight, offering support with his body as his other arm held her waist.

Sparks of pleasure jolted to every cell in her body, setting them aflame before pooling into tiny pulses of bliss. Small whimpers escaped her throat, laced with her unyielding desire for him as she gave herself to the only man she'd ever loved.

Sebastian held her until her quivers abated, continuing to place soft kisses on her ear and temple. Slowly regaining her wits, she lifted her head, opening her eyes but finding it hard to focus. His low-toned laugh surrounded her as he nudged her nose with his.

"Are you...*laughing* at me?" she almost squeaked. "Goddess, Sebastian, I'm already so embarrassed...please don't make it worse."

"Embarrassed you came?" he asked, eyebrows drawing together and his hand clenching her mound. "Why would you be embarrassed about that, darling?"

The endearment reminded her of their night together, and of how he'd showered tender words on someone who wasn't truly her. Feeling her heart crack, she lowered her gaze, unable to meet his eyes.

"Because you want me because you're angry and nothing more. I know what you think of me, Sebastian."

Tilting her chin, he reclaimed her gaze as tangible energy pulsed between them. Those limitless eyes darted between hers, seeming to contemplate before he slowly lifted his hand from her mound. Lifting it to his mouth, he glided his tongue over his finger, licking away her essence before moving to the next one.

"Tell me, darling," he rasped, eyes locked with hers as he licked her honey from his fingers. "Tell me as I taste your release on my fingers what I really think of you."

Mesmerized by his sensual actions, Celine could only watch as he licked every glistening drop from his hand. Then he stepped forward, aligning his lips with hers before plunging his tongue into her mouth.

He kissed her, languid and deep, and she tasted herself on his tongue. Breaking the kiss, he drew back and licked his lips, the gesture so erotic she felt a new rush of wetness at her core.

"You think I'm boring...and cold...and insignificant..." she finished lamely.

"Mmm..." was his sultry reply as he continued to lick his lips. "What else?"

"Damn you," she whispered, wishing she could release his shoulders but needing the stronghold to stay upright. "Stop mocking me!"

Cocking a brow, his lips curled into a sexy grin. "You deserve much worse than mockery, my dear, but I find myself unable to be angry at you right now. I'd take the win."

Exhaling a breath, the guilt rushed over her once more. "I'm sorry for deceiving you, Sebastian. Truly, I am. I hope you don't hate me."

"Hate is very far from the emotion I'm feeling right now," he muttered. "Most importantly, I'm wondering how in the hell I was so blind." Trailing his fingers over her hair, he gazed at her reverently as her heart pounded. "I knew your hair felt coarse that night...you wore a wig."

Biting her lip, she nodded.

"And I consider myself an observant person. Guess that's out the window."

Taking pity on him, she laughed and cupped his jaw. "I knew you wouldn't notice. It was me after all."

Sighing, he shook his head. "I'm going to need some time to process what an oblivious idiot I am."

"I'm just happy you're not still yelling. I've created a bit of a mess."

"I would argue we both have—"

The door to Mila's office swung open and Handor stepped inside. "Mila, have you seen Celine? I need her for—" Bristling, his mouth fell open as he observed their sensual position on the desk, Sebastian between his daughter's open legs as her skirt fell to one side.

"You son of a bitch!" he hissed, jabbing his finger at Sebastian. "How dare you touch my daughter before she bonds?"

"Father!" she cried, mourning the loss of Sebastian's warm body as he drew away. Repositioning her gown over her legs, she hopped to her feet and smoothed it over her thighs. "This is none of your concern!"

"None of my concern?" His face turned a thousand shades of red as his eyes threatened to bulge from his head. "Your one duty is to bond with a suitable mate, and I find you here, giving yourself to someone who hasn't promised you anything?"

"I'm sorry, Handor," Sebastian said, showing his palm. "I take full responsibility."

"Damn right you do. I demand you bond with her. If you have any honor, you'll set things right."

Alarmed at the escalation, Celine held up her hands. "Enough! No one is bonding with anyone. Everyone needs to calm down—"

"I agree, sir," Sebastian interrupted, appearing contrite. "I will bond with Celine."

"What?" she cried, not understanding how things had devolved so quickly. Of course, she'd always dreamed of bonding with Sebastian, but not if he was forced to do it. No—this was all wrong. He was supposed to fall madly in love with her before lowering to one knee and asking her to be his mate for eternity...

A slight bit of tension left Handor's shoulders as he warily eyed Sebastian. "Fine. We will have the ceremony next weekend. There's no time to waste since she is compromised."

"Compromised!" she exclaimed, stomping her foot. "I'm right here! Stop speaking as if I don't exist. No one is bonding next weekend—"

"Yes, sir," Sebastian said, "I am honored to have Celine as my bonded mate."

Ending the discussion, her father nodded and turned to leave the office. "Have your father contact me so we can work out the details, Sebastian. If I know Astaroth, he'll want to have the ceremony in his back yard to keep up appearances."

Scoffing at how alike their fathers were, Celine gaped at Sebastian. "Are you really going to let this happen?"

"You have no choice, Celine," her father said, his tone devoid of emotion. "I won't have a daughter so careless with her choices under my roof any longer. You can begin packing when you return home so your things are ready to move to Sebastian's home after the ceremony." With a final nod, he strode through the door, closing it behind him.

Swiping a hand through her hair, she stared open-mouthed at the door as Sebastian stood silent. Shaking her hands with exasperation, she approached him. "You can't be serious. This is mad-ness, Sebastian."

Unreadable eyes lifted to hers, swirling with emotions she couldn't begin to decipher. "It's done, Celine. Let's make the best of it."

Sputtering, she slapped her palm to her forehead. "Make the *best* of it? Up until twenty minutes ago, you didn't even know I existed, and *now* you want to bond with me? This is absurd."

Raw emotion laced his features as a muscle ticked in his jaw. "As I stated, I was a fool. A fact I am now trying to remedy."

"From one night together where you didn't know it was me and one tiny moment of passion?" She gestured to Mila's desk. "Absolutely not. This isn't the way it's supposed to happen, Sebastian. We can't—"

Striding toward her, he gripped her arms, careful but firm. "Your father saw us in a compromising position, Celine. We have no other option." Lifting his hand, he splayed his fingers and leaned forward, speaking in a low growl. "And now that my fingers have been buried inside your sweet body, you're insane if you think I'll allow anyone else to touch you."

A disbelieving laugh escaped her lips. "You've had centuries to bond with me, Sebastian. *Centuries!*"

His lips thinned as he spared her a droll look. "My dear, I'm sure you know this, but men are often daft. I have no excuse except to say I'm a workaholic who never saw much beyond the horizon of my desk. A feat I wish to remedy immediately."

Feeling her chin wobble, she shook her head. "This isn't how it's supposed to happen. It can't happen this way..."

Confusion marred his features as tears formed in her eyes.

"Oh, you'll never understand," she warbled, pressing her fist to her lips. "Goddess, what have I done?" Unable to face him any longer—or to accept her inevitable fate—a sob escaped her throat as she pivoted to leave.

"Celine, please—"

"No," she said, shaking her arm from his grasp. "It can't happen like this. I won't let it. I have to speak to my father." Gathering her skirt in her fists, she burst through the door to try to talk some sense into the hardheaded man.

Once home, she begged and pleaded with Handor for hours to no avail. He was determined to bond her to Sebastian and complete his duty to find a worthy bonded mate. In that moment, she truly understood she'd never represented anything more than a brood mare and a burden to him.

Climbing the stairs on shaking legs, she threw herself on her bed and wept at the knowledge she was destined to bond with a man who didn't love her back and most likely never would. If he'd been granted the chance to court her after their passionate tryst on the desk, perhaps she could've wormed her way under his stoic exterior and carved off a small piece of his heart.

But, alas, she'd run out of time, and she would now become a duty and a burden to the man who'd never seen her and who now had no incentive to even try.

Chapter 10

S ebastian lowered to Mila's desk, perching on it as he rubbed his forehead. The past hour had quite certainly been the most eventful of his life, and he doubted there would ever be one to rival it. He'd discovered Celine's treachery, realized the woman he'd been obsessed with for the past week was one he'd known for centuries, shared an intimately erotic moment with said woman, and agreed to bond with her.

Yes, quite eventful indeed.

For someone as commitment-phobic as Sebastian, he should've been furious at Handor's demand he bond with Celine. And yet, as soon as the declaration had left her father's mouth, Sebastian had rushed to agree. Why? Contemplating, he rubbed his chin.

Because something changed last weekend, and you know it.

Narrowing his eyes, Sebastian accepted the very obvious truth. Something *had* shifted when he saw Anya—saw *Celine*—standing tall and regal in the moonlight. A piece of his heart that was locked away had been set free, and he'd become open to possibilities he'd never considered. Hell, he'd even told Mila he thought she was his mate. His friend's resounding smirk should've been yet another clue that his phantom lover wasn't a phantom after all.

Goddess, he was an oblivious fool.

"Well?" Mila asked, striding into the office. "Where's Celine?"

"I assume she's speaking with her father, begging him to end the betrothal we entered into."

Stopping short, Mila worked her jaw. "You're betrothed to Handor?"

"Funny," he said, his expression droll. "Handor burst through the door looking for Celine when we were...uh...compromised."

"Oh, wow," Mila said, eyes alight with excitement. "How compromised?"

Glancing at the desk, he arched a brow. "Pretty compromised."

"Ew," she said, striding toward the desk and shooing him away. "Do I need to disinfect something?"

Breathing a laugh, he shook his head. "I think you're fine. But it was comprising enough that Handor demanded I bond with her." Tilting his head, his features drew together. "And before I knew it, I agreed. In fact, I couldn't get the 'yes' through my lips fast enough." Lifting his gaze to Mila's, he swallowed thickly. "What the hell does that mean?"

"Oh, my dear friend," she said, approaching and patting his shoulder. "I think it means you've finally met your match. It's the only reason I agreed to her scheme. I saw the logic of you both shaking things up. You just needed a change of perspective to see what was in front of you both."

"Thanks for that, by the way," he muttered. "I feel like an idiot. How did I not know it was her?"

Lowering into the chair, she shrugged. "Celine was raised to blend into the background. To be a dutiful, biddable female. But times have changed, and she desperately wants the world to see her for who she truly is." Her lips formed a soft smile. "She wants *you* to see her that way most of all. I think Saturday was the first time you let down your walls and allowed that to happen."

Sitting beside her, he reclined in the chair as he pondered. "I should be pissed, and a part of me is, but another part of me is grateful she took the chance." Leaning forward, he rested his forearms on his thighs. "I've never felt like this, Mila. It's daunting...and also quite...magnificent."

"Well, you're welcome." Crossing her ankle over her knee, she shook her foot as she spoke. "Just remember, she's quite sheltered and has no way to survive on her own. It will take time to fully realize her potential once she's escaped from Handor's grip. You could be the one who helps her grow, Sebastian. You're so altruistic with our people, and you could show a bit of that consideration to her once you bond."

"I can," he said with a nod. "Although, she seemed...disappointed. I guess I thought..."

"Yes?"

"Well, she must have feelings for me if she concocted this scheme, right?"

Arching a brow, Mila muttered, "What do you think?"

Scowling, he asked, "Then why wouldn't she be happy to bond with me?"

"Well, let's see." Ticking her fingers, Mila said, "She's had feelings for you for centuries, which you completely ignored. She finally gathers the courage to do something about it and gets caught by her father doing the nasty with you. Her father demands you bond with her and a business transaction is made between you." Her features turned sardonic. "Did she have *any* say in the matter?"

"I..." Scratching his head, he frowned. "Well, not really. I just assumed she would find me an acceptable match. I mean, seconds earlier, she was moaning my name on your desk—"

"TMI," Mila interjected, holding up a hand. "You didn't even ask her, did you? No sweet words or romanticism at all."

"No," was his sullen reply as began to realize why Celine was upset.

Sighing, she shook her head. "Men. Every last one of you are idiots."

"I get it." Holding up a hand, he nodded. "She deserves better."

"She deserves *more* than better." Rising, she tapped his forehead. "Search your brain for how to do that, Sebastian. I think you could build an amazing life together, but you're going to have to figure out how to be a good mate."

Standing, he cupped her shoulder. "You're putting a lot of faith in a man who never wanted a commitment."

"Until now. Don't lie to yourself. She's under your skin. I've never seen you like this."

Unable to stop his smile, he nodded. "She's definitely under my skin. It feels good. I didn't expect that."

"Love and bonding are never duties or chores if you're with the right person. Look at your brother with Siora. He's completely besotted with her and happily so. That's how true love works."

Blowing a breath through his lips, Sebastian shook his head. "Avowals of love are still too terrifying to contemplate, but I'll admit, Celine has awakened something in me. I've never been a coward, Mila, and I want to pursue this."

"No, you haven't. Now go fix this mess you two created. Give her some romance, Sebastian. You can do it."

"I'm still half-pissed at you," he teased, holding his thumb and forefinger an inch apart.

"Good. Maybe you'll leave me alone so I can work." Shooing him away, she trailed behind her desk. "Gotta get back to it. Congrats on the betrothal. Byeeeee!" Lowering to the chair, she faced the computer and began to type.

Realizing he'd been dismissed, Sebastian left the office and headed down the sidewalk. Pulling out his phone, he called his brother.

"Hey," Garridan's deep voice chimed. "I'm about to head into training, but I have five minutes. What's up?"

"I think it's time I finally took possession of your key," Sebastian said. "I know you offered for me to move into your house now that you've moved to Lynia, but I never saw the need to."

"And now you do?"

Clearing his throat, Sebastian inhaled a deep breath. "Now I do. You see, I've recently become betrothed."

His brother must've been drinking water because a choking noise sounded over the phone before he broke into a coughing fit. Sebastian couldn't help but grin at his obvious surprise.

"Excuse me," he said after the coughing abated, "I must be hearing things. It sounded like you said you were betrothed."

"I am."

Garridan's palpable confusion emanated through the phone. "And who is the lucky lady?"

Grinning from ear to ear, Sebastian wondered if his brother would break into another fit of coughing at the news. "Celine."

Silence drifted between them.

"Garridan?"

"I'm waiting to hear the punchline. Don't get me wrong, I'd love nothing more than for you to bond with Celine. I always thought she was perfect for you, brother. But you barely ever noticed her. And believe me, we tried."

His eyebrows drew together. "What the hell does that mean?"

"Remember the fundraiser before the battle with Bakari? I offered to be her wingman to try to make you jealous. Of course, it didn't work because you spent most of the night holed up in your office working."

"My council work is important, Garridan."

"I know, but it won't keep you warm at night, brother. I wager Celine will be much better at that.

Trust me. Having Siora at my side means more than any medal or promotion I've ever achieved."

"Aww," Siora chimed in the background. "He's so sweet. Hope he remembers that when I kick his ass in this drill we're about to start. Come on, no time to chitchat."

Sebastian heard a smacking sound, which he assumed was Siora placing a firm kiss on his brother's lips, before Garridan chuckled. "Goddess, I love her. Have to go. I'll bring the key to you when I'm done in a few hours. There are a few basic items left in the house, and I hope you'll decorate it and make it your own. I'm happy for you, Sebastian."

"I'll tell you the whole story when I see you. Let's just say there's a lot more to Celine than meets the eye."

Garridan's chuckle echoed over the phone. "It's finally time you figured that out. I like Celine immensely and will be honored to call her family. Well done."

"Don't congratulate me yet. She's not exactly thrilled. I'm going to need some pointers from you on romance and whatever else women like."

"Garridan!" Siora called in the background. "Get your ass over her and stop wasting my time!"

"As you can see, I'm no expert either," Garridan muttered. "But the best advice I can give you is to put her first. If you do that, she'll give you the world. Gotta go. See you later."

The phone went dead as Sebastian took his brother's words to heart. *Put her first.* Hell, he was an altruistic council member who put his constituents first every day. He certainly could do it with the woman who'd burrowed under his skin and turned his world upside down in a matter of days. She deserved nothing less, and as he strolled under the midday sun, he made a silent promise to give it to her.

Chapter 11

T he next day, Celine was in the sitting room anxiously chewing her nail as she wondered if she would ever regain control of her own damn life. A knock sounded at the front door, startling her, and she trailed through the foyer before slowly pulling it open.

Sebastian stood on the other side, so handsome in his crisp white-collared shirt and dress pants. A few springy brown hairs peeked from beneath the shirt below his neck, and her mouth suddenly went dry as she had visions of kissing him there. Would the hairs tickle her lips as she went lower?

"Hi," he said, his tone warm as he smiled. "Are you busy?"

"Busy watching my life fall apart," she muttered, arching a brow. "Why?"

His smile deepened as his eyes roved over her face. "I'd like to show you something." Extending his hand, he waited. "If you're willing to come with me."

Narrowing her eyes, she studied his hand. "Aren't you supposed to be working? You *are* the most infamous workaholic on the compound."

Chuckling, he nodded. "I am, but I find something else...or rather, *someone* else, has captured my attention recently." Affection swam in his eyes as he shook his hand. "Please?"

Taken by his adorable grin and tender plea, Celine took his hand, closing the door behind her. They began to walk down the sidewalk, and she realized he was leading her to his home several blocks away.

"Where are we going?"

Evading her question, he surveyed her formal gown. It was a deep purple that highlighted her pale complexion. "You look very pretty today."

"Compliments will get you nowhere, especially since I've worn this gown a thousand times and you've never noticed."

His lips twitched. "I'm noticing now."

Huffing a breath, she remained silent, wishing she wasn't thrilled to be in his presence. In truth, it was wonderful to have his full attention after craving it for so long, but she'd be damned if she let him know that. He was no better than her father, trading her as if she were a baseball card between human teenagers. Just dreadful.

They arrived at Astaroth's home, and Sebastian led her down a private walkway to the house on the adjacent property. Garridan had lived there for centuries before he recently moved to Lynia to be with Siora.

"You're taking me to your brother's home?"

He didn't answer, leading her to the front door and inserting a key to unlock it. Drawing her inside, they walked down a long hallway to a living room with large windows, a couch, and a fireplace.

"As you can see, it's pretty sparse. Garridan only left a few items—the couch, some chairs, the bed." His eyes lit with desire. "But otherwise, it's going to need to be decorated."

"You're moving in here?"

Clasping her hands in his, he squeezed. "*We're* moving in here. If you agree, of course."

"I wasn't aware I had a choice," was her sardonic reply as she scanned the room.

"Celine, I'm sorry I didn't ask you. It was a precarious situation, and I reacted without thinking." Lifting her chin with his fingers, he gazed into her eyes. "And neither of us is perfect here, darling. If you recall, you deceived me. Quite viciously—"

"It wasn't vicious," she interjected, heart pounding from the warmth of his fingers. "I just...wanted to know how it felt to be near you and have you notice me," she finished lamely, dropping her gaze in embarrassment.

"Mission accomplished," he said, arching a teasing brow. "And I don't want our mistakes to linger between us. I'll forgive you for deceiving me if you forgive me for being an unromantic dolt and not *asking* you to bond with me."

Swallowing thickly, she pondered. "I don't want to bond with someone who doesn't want me, Sebastian."

A tender light entered his gaze as he cupped her jaw, slowly running his thumb over her cheek. "Your father has made his decision, Celine. He's determined we bond, and whether it's fair or not, you don't have any recourse. You're dependent on him and have no way to support yourself if we don't bond."

Tears filled her eyes as she silently accepted his words.

"But I can help you, if you'll let me. I have no wish to rob you of your independence. I want to help you gain it."

Her eyebrows drew together. "And how will I do that if we're bonded? My ownership will just transfer from my father to you."

"I have no wish to own you, darling." Glancing at the ceiling, Sebastian squinted one eye. "Except, perhaps, in the bedroom." Reclaiming her gaze, a naughty glint entered his eyes. "But we can discuss that later. For now, I want a partner. An equal."

Pretending her body wasn't thrumming from his "bedroom" comment, she toyed with her lip with her fangs. "An equal how?"

"I'll give you a stipend each month—yours to save and spend however you like. If you detest being bonded to me, eventually, you can take it all and leave."

A shocked laugh left her throat. "You're joking."

"I'm one hundred percent serious, my dear," he said, lifting a finger. "I hope this will assure you that bonding with me won't be quite as dreadful as you've decided."

Her gaze fell to his chest, roaming his crisp shirt as she mulled over his proposal. "You're still purchasing me in a way. But I guess I have no other choice." Clearing her throat, she battled the shyness that warred within. "And we'll be…intimate?"

Cupping her chin, he waited until she reclaimed his gaze. "Yes, Celine. You said you didn't want to bond with a man who didn't want you, but I'm pretty sure you were in Mila's office yesterday." Stepping closer, he pressed his body to hers. "I think it's quite obvious I want you, darling."

Her treacherous body strained toward his muscular one, reveling in the feel of his taut muscles and firm length against her stomach. Licking her lips, her knees wobbled at the flare of lust in his eyes.

"I want to bond with someone who loves me, Sebastian," she whispered.

Running his thumb over her lip, he formed a gentle smile. "I understand." Inhaling deeply, he slowly shook his head. "I don't want there to be anything but honesty between us. An avowal of love at this point would be disingenuous, and you deserve better than that, Celine."

A tiny crack shot through her heart.

"This is still very new, and I've been a confirmed bachelor for centuries. But..." Lifting a finger, he cocked his brow. "I'm willing to try. Give me some time. Let me earn you. I'm open to love, but I have a lot to learn. Maybe you can help me."

His expression was earnest as he softly caressed her jaw, and she knew in that moment she would never love another. He was offering her freedom and the chance to build a life with him. Moreover, he desired her and was blatantly honest. It was more than most women had in these circumstances, and if she opened her heart to him, perhaps he would do the same. Inhaling a huge breath, she opened her mouth and spoke the words that would cement her future.

"I would be honored to be your partner, Sebastian. It's a lovely offer. Thank you."

Relief washed over his handsome features as he palmed both of her cheeks. "Thank the goddess." Leaning forward, he brushed his lips over hers. "I'm honored to have you, Celine. Now kiss me to seal the deal."

Shivering from his command, she slid her arms around his neck, drawing him into a heated kiss. He moaned as his tongue glided over hers, sending a jolt of wetness to her core. Maneuvering his lips over hers, he spoke hungrily into her mouth.

"I can't wait to be inside you," he rasped, threading his fingers through her hair as he plundered her mouth. "I'll be a proper gentleman and wait until our bonding night, but know that I'm going to ravish you afterward, darling." Waggling his brows, he nipped her lip. "Maybe you should decorate the bedroom first."

Laughing, she glanced around the room. "The house definitely needs a lot of work."

"I'll leave that to you. It's your home now, and I want you to decorate it however you see fit."

Joy surged through her at the thought of owning something and putting her stamp on it. "Are you sure?"

"Absolutely." He pecked her lips. "Just nothing too pink. Otherwise, go for it."

"I like purples and deep greens...and a royal blue here and there. I'll figure it out. What's the budget?"

Arching a brow, he shrugged. "In case you haven't noticed, I'm the eldest son of an aristocrat who's richer than half the kingdom combined. I also make a good salary as a council member. So I say go for it. The sky's the limit."

Biting her lip, she grinned. "Are you placating me with decorating so I'll be amenable to you in the bedroom?"

"Why, Celine, you wound my heart," he teased, covering his chest with his palm. "And also, yes. Very much yes."

Giggling, she nodded. "I'll allow it. Oh, Sebastian, this will be fun! Thank you!"

His expression was reverent as he tucked a strand of hair behind her ear. "I like seeing you smile. I think I might have to buy more houses for you to decorate."

"Oh, stop." She swatted his chest as he chuckled. Licking her lips, she said softly, "I'm looking forward to our bonding night. I'd gotten to the point where I was afraid I was never going to lose my virginity."

His frame shuddered in her arms, and she glowed with the knowledge that he was viscerally attracted to her, even if he didn't love her. Although her gala-night scheme had unintended consequences, she was finally able to admit it had been worth it.

"Oh, it's as good as gone, darling." Leaning down, he pressed his lips to her ear. "I'm going to bury myself so deep inside you there will be no doubt who you belong to."

Shivering in anticipation, she clutched him, hoping she would be able to please him when the time came. He held her for a small eternity, whispering sweet words in her ear as they gently swayed. Accepting her future, she closed her eyes and vowed to ensure she did everything in her power to make him love her back.

Chapter 12

A week later, Sebastian stood in his father's expansive back yard under a white altar lined with flowers. The sun shone brightly above, and a bead of sweat dripped down his temple. After wiping it away with his sleeve, he stuck his finger between his collar and neck, attempting to create some space. Damn, but it was tight.

"Stop fidgeting," Garridan muttered behind him, causing Sebastian to glower. "You're going to be fine, brother. Deep breaths."

"You can skip the unwanted 'best man advice,'" he said, scowling. "Never in a million years did I think I'd bond first, but here we are."

"It's time, Sebastian," Garridan said, patting his arm. "You were hiding behind your job, just as I was hiding behind my position in the army before I met

Siora. Your life is about to become so much fuller. I can't wait to see it."

The officiant—a well-respected retired councilman who was friends with Astaroth—cleared his throat, and Sebastian straightened his shoulders, facing the altar. As he waited for Celine to walk down the aisle, he begrudgingly admitted his brother's words were true.

For so long, he'd hidden behind his duty, telling himself it was noble. Yes, his job helped people, and he took immense pride in that. But he would be lying to himself if he didn't admit his life had become quite...hollow. A shell of the full life he promised himself he'd live one day but hadn't pursued in centuries. Somewhere along the way, he'd just accepted the status quo and forgotten to take the next steps.

His lips twitched as admiration for Celine surged within. She'd been quite stagnant too, but she'd taken it upon herself to try something different. Although he'd been shocked to discover she was his mystery lover, he admitted it had jump-started both their lives in a new direction. And for once, he was *excited* about something.

After so many years of wearing blinders, he was beginning to see Celine for the woman she was. Feisty and brave when she summoned her inner courage, but still innocent and sheltered in other ways. Thanks to Miranda and Evie, women in their realm were no longer background characters in aristocratic men's lives, and Celine would benefit from having a partner instead of a caretaker like her father.

Sebastian didn't know the first thing about relationships, but he felt they could grow into one together. She could relieve him of his habit of being a stuffy workaholic, and he could give her autonomy to make her own choices. Although he'd sworn he didn't want a bonded mate, he realized he was grateful to Etherya for the circumstances that had led him here. Yes, he was nervous, but that was normal for any man about to bond. But he finally understood what others had seen for so long: he and Celine were an excellent match.

Music emanated from the string quartet situated beside the rows of chairs, and he turned to face Celine as she glided down the white carpet. *Oohs* and *ahhs* emanated from the crowd as they rose, the guests' reactions reflecting the consensus: his mate was absolutely radiant.

She grinned at him from behind her veil, nervously biting her lip, and he winked as all remaining hesitation left his body. If he had to bond with anyone, he was grateful it was this gorgeous woman who embodied so much more passion and character than most would ever know. Hell, he'd overlooked her for centuries because he'd bought into the narrative everyone wrote about Celine. They were all fools—he the biggest one of all—but she'd pulled back the curtain and showed him her true essence.

She approached, kissing her father's cheek before he released her and sat in the front row. Taking her hands, Sebastian squeezed, resolved to do right by her and make the best of their circumstances. Turning to face the officiant, he held her hand as they recited the vows of Etherya in front of their friends and family.

After a long day of dancing and celebrating, the last guests departed Astaroth's property and Celine lifted a hand to her mouth to stifle a yawn.

"Tired, darling?" Sebastian asked, sliding his arm around her waist.

"Yes. Bonding ceremonies are exhausting. I might have to stay with you forever just so I never have to do this again."

Chuckling, he kissed her temple. "I'm happy to hear one more reason you won't rush to leave me. It would ruin my reputation."

Wrinkling her nose at his teasing, she smiled as his parents approached.

"All the guests are gone, and we're heading to bed," Astaroth said, shaking Sebastian's hand before turning to Celine. "Thank you for finally convincing my son to bond." Cupping Sebastian's shoulder, he beamed. "I expect an heir soon."

"On that note, we're heading home," Sebastian droned. "I know it's been your greatest wish to see me bonded for centuries. Let's take the win and hold off on the 'heir' talk for a few months at least." Kissing his mother on the cheek, he faced Celine. "Ready?"

Nodding, she kissed his parents goodbye, thanking them for their hospitality as hosts, and slipped her hand in Sebastian's. He led them across the property to his home—their home now—and stopped at the front door. Pushing it open, he lowered, gathering her in his arms as she yelped. Chuckling, he carried her over the threshold before setting her on her feet.

"I messed up the proposal, but at least I can do one thing right."

Celine smiled at his thoughtfulness before slipping off her shoes and massaging her tired feet. "I can't wear those things one more minute. My feet are throbbing."

Approaching her, he slipped an arm around her waist. "I'm happy to relieve you of any clothing that is causing you distress, dear."

Her heart slammed in her chest as he gazed at her with lust-filled eyes. Tiny butterflies of anxiety fluttered in her belly, and she did her best to tamp them down. "How very thoughtful," she rasped.

"You have no idea," he murmured, cocking a brow. "But you will soon. Let me lock up and I'll be right up."

Nodding, she trailed up the stairs, entering the bedroom she'd begun to decorate days ago. After their conversation, she'd seen no reason to wait to start making the home her own. Plus, she'd known they were going to need the bedroom decorated for their bonding night, so she'd already spruced up the room with new bedding and furniture.

Sitting at the new vanity she'd purchased, Celine observed her reflection as she removed her earrings before starting to pluck the various pins out of her hair.

Sebastian entered the room, removing his jacket and tossing it onto the nearby chair.

"I did *not* purchase that chair to be a clothes hanger," she teasingly scolded. "I hope you're not one of those men who don't hang their clothes."

Grinning, he approached, lithe as a cougar as he slowly unbuttoned his shirt. "I'm afraid I've been a bachelor too long." Removing the shirt, he tossed it across the room to lie atop his jacket. "Perhaps you'll punish me for my transgressions."

Choppy breaths exited her lungs as she gazed at him in the reflection. "Perhaps."

She continued to remove the pins, shaking her hair so it fell loose and full down her back.

Placing his hands on her shoulders, Sebastian asked, "Do you need help with your dress?"

Swallowing thickly, she nodded and rose. Pushing the bench under the vanity, she presented her back to him. Sweeping her hair over one shoulder, she grinned over the other one. "The buttons are tiny. Let me know if you can't release them."

His deft fingers freed the tiny pearls one by one, and his skill sent shards of doubt through her frame. How many lovers had he been with? Did she have a chance of pleasing him since she had no experience at all?

After all the buttons were free, he pushed the fabric open, and a waft of cold air rushed against her back. Stepping forward, he traced his finger over the birthmark at the juncture of her neck and shoulder.

"I remember kissing this pretty mark the night of the gala," he said, his caress causing heat to flare in her belly. "I promised myself I would do it again one day."

Shuddering at his visceral words, she closed her eyes. "Sebastian..."

"Like this," he murmured, gliding his arm around her waist and aligning his front with her backside. Lowering his mouth to the mark, he tenderly kissed it.

Tilting her head, she allowed him access, loving the feel of his lips against her skin. He kissed her affectionately before lowering his hand to cup the mound of her sex through her dress. Burying his nose in her neck, he inhaled deeply.

"Goddess, Celine," he murmured, scraping his fangs against her neck as her knees buckled. "You smell so good. How did I never notice?"

"I think you have to be within several feet of someone to notice their scent," she teased, glancing at him in the reflection.

Lust flared in his eyes. "I plan to be wrapped around you all night, darling, so that won't be a problem." Stepping back, he slowly pushed her dress down her body so it pooled at her feet.

She stood before him, clad only in her strapless bra and thong, and fought the urge to cover herself.

"Oh no," he said, grasping her hand and leading her to the bed. "You're not allowed to cover one inch of flesh when it's bared to me." Turning her, his lips formed a salacious smile. "I want to see every part of you, Celine."

Tears welled in her eyes as the backs of her knees brushed the bed. She'd waited so long to be right here, but now that the time had come, nerves flared in her chest.

"Darling?" he asked, brushing a tendril of hair from her temple. "What's wrong?"

"I..." Swallowing thickly, she shook her head. "I have no idea how to please you. I've always hated my virginity, and never more than right now."

Compassion crossed his expression as he gently encircled her hand, drawing it to his swollen shaft underneath his pants. Celine caressed him, tenderly squeezing as he groaned.

Leaning forward, he nipped her bottom lip. "As you can see, I am sufficiently pleased."

A soft giggle escaped her throat. "But we haven't even started."

"The fun is in the buildup, dear. Would you like me to show you?"

Unable to reply, she slowly nodded.

"Good girl."

The words sent shivers through her frame.

"Lie down," he instructed, tugging her toward the bed.

Celine lay on her back, shimmying up the comforter until her head rested on the pillow. Fanning her hair to spread across the satin, she waited.

Sebastian placed the pad of his finger on her collarbone, trailing it down her body, over the fabric of her bra, and down her belly. Her skin quivered underneath as he placed his palm over her abdomen.

"I'm a bit dominant, if you hadn't noticed." His fingers caressed her skin, soothing her as he spoke. "I think you like it, judging by the way you respond to me." His hand drifted lower to play with the lacy hem of her panties. "But if I do or say anything you don't like, I want you to tell me. Do you understand?"

She nodded.

"Give me the words, sweetheart."

"I understand."

His lips curved into a sultry smile as he lightly tapped the hood of her mound several times. Celine squirmed on the bed, her hips arching to meet his hand, craving more.

"Goddess, you're so responsive. I love that about you, darling."

Celine's heart melted at the poignant words. Although not a declaration of love, they were caring and sensual, and they quelled a large portion of the doubt that simmered in her belly.

Removing his hand, he stepped back, eyes locked with hers as he discarded his clothes. Naked, he strode forward, and Celine couldn't help but study him. Small brown hairs covered his chest under broad shoulders, leading to a narrow waist and muscular thighs. His sex stood tall and proud from his body, reaching for her as it seemed to pulse in the dim light of the bedside lamp. His thighs brushed the bed before he palmed his length, sliding his hand back and forth as his breaths grew heavy.

"This is for you, Celine," he murmured, stroking his cock as he gazed into her eyes. "You already please me more than you know."

She lay frozen, mesmerized by his words and the erotic motion of his hand.

"There's nothing you need to do except let me love you, darling. Now, raise your hands above your head."

Dazed by his sultry tone, she lifted her arms, resting them on the pillow as his nostrils flared with desire.

Climbing onto the bed, he straddled her, his thick cock resting on her abdomen as his eyes darted over her bare flesh. Gliding his hands under her back, he unclasped her bra, lifting it in the air and shaking it.

"I'm going to toss it on the floor. Don't scold me."

Breathing a laugh, she shook her head. "I won't."

Winking, he tossed it to the carpet before placing his palms on her stomach. Desire marked his handsome features as he slowly slid his palms toward her breasts. Cupping the small mounds, he squeezed, groaning as he palmed her flesh.

"They're quite small," she said, biting her lip. "Sometimes I wish I were curvier like Mila—"

"You're perfect," he interjected, lowering to brush a kiss across her lips. "Now, hush and let me kiss you."

Celine licked her lips, preparing for the onslaught from his mouth.

Chuckling, he shook his head and placed his lips against her collarbone. "Not there," he rasped, trailing kisses over the valley between her breasts before veering sideways toward her nipple. "Let me kiss you here." Grazing the little bud with his lips, he gauged her reaction.

"*Oh, goddess...*" she whispered, watching her nipple grow taut and turgid as he grinned. "*Please...*"

Opening his mouth, he placed it over her nipple, drawing it inside as she squirmed beneath him. The wet warmth of his tongue washed over her, and she mewled, pressing into him.

"*Mmmm...*" he moaned, cupping her other breast as his mouth created the sweetest suction on her nipple. "Do you like that, sweetheart?"

"Yes!" she cried, clutching the pillow above her head, leaving her hands high as he commanded although she desperately wanted to clutch his hair.

"And how about this?" Extending his tongue, he flicked the taut nub over and over as heat flushed every cell of her skin. Drowning in pleasure, she purred, feeling the tingle between her thighs as wetness rushed to her core.

His tongue and fingers toyed with her nipples before he switched, kissing a path to the other breast and laving it with his tongue. He sucked and flicked her in an endless rhythm as his fingers toyed with the wet pointed nipple his mouth had abandoned. Writhing under him, Celine felt a burning deep in her belly.

"You're on fire for me, aren't you, sweetness?" he growled, sucking her nipple deep into his mouth as she squirmed. "Let me taste how much you want me. Goddess, I'm dying to taste you…"

His mouth placed wet kisses down her stomach as he repositioned himself between her legs. Hooking his fingers beneath the straps of her thong, he quickly tugged it off her quivering body. Cupping the backs of her knees, Sebastian placed them over his shoulders. Embarrassment swelled as he faced her deepest place, and her legs reflexively attempted to draw together.

"Oh, no," he commanded, pushing her thighs wider with his shoulders as he placed his fingers on her wet folds. "You'll bare this sweet pussy to me, Celine. Do you hear me?"

"Yes," she whispered, instinctively arching toward his mouth.

His sultry chuckle surrounded her. Drawing her folds open, he blew a long, warm breath over her core. Staring deep into her eyes, he asked softly, "Yes, what?"

Groaning, her back arched on the mattress.

"Don't deny me, darling. Follow your instincts. Your submission is addictive to someone like me, and so damn beautiful." Blowing on her center again, he waited. "Yes what, Celine?"

"Yes, sir."

His large frame shuddered between her legs, causing her to realize how much her submission pleased him. Understanding dawned as she comprehended that submission didn't mean lack of control. Instead, she suddenly felt drunk on her own arousal...and on the power she had to make him tremble with need. Pushing toward him, she offered herself, unabashed and unafraid.

A ragged groan escaped his throat before he lowered his head, nuzzling into her wet slit. Locking his gaze with hers, he licked a path from her slick opening, over her sensitive folds, to the tiny nub at the top of her sex. Overcome with joy, she closed her eyes, head falling back on the pillow as he loved her.

His deep murmurs of approval vibrated against her wet skin as he lapped up her essence, licking every spot on her core until she felt the orgasm looming on the horizon.

"Please, Sebastian. I need to move my arms...I need to touch you..."

"You're such a good girl to ask me nicely, Celine," he murmured against her wet folds. "You can move your arms, darling."

Whimpering, she lowered her arms, thrusting her fingers in his hair and clenching. Unbridled lust burned within as she drew him deeper, begging for more as he growled against her. Closing his lips over her clit, he began to suck...then flick...then suck once more...causing the engorged bud to swell even more under his intense ministrations.

"Oh god, right there," she crooned, spearing her nails into his scalp as he stimulated her clit with his tongue. "Oh...*Sebastian*...I'm going to come..."

He spread her folds wider, his mouth working the sensitive nub until her spine stiffened.

Giving in to the orgasm, she expelled a shuddered moan, her body racking with tremors as pleasure shot from the base of her spine to every cell in her frame. Riding the wave, she reveled in his words of approval whispered against her wet, ravaged core as he nuzzled into her. For so long, she'd dreamed of having Sebastian desire her. Finally, after so many centuries, he was hers. Reveling in her love for him, she tightened her thighs, hugging him closer as her muscles quivered.

His deep laugh reverberated against her, and she opened one eye, squinting down at him. Small quakes shook her frame as she gave him an incredulous look. "Are you really laughing at me? Seriously, Sebastian, you're going to give me a complex."

Running the tip of his nose over her wet folds and inner thigh, his lips formed a lascivious grin. "I'm sorry, sweetheart. You were squeezing me with your thighs and I had the fleeting thought I might be smothered by your sweet pussy." Kissing her mound, his grin deepened. "And I quickly realized that's the only way I want to go if I ever meet my untimely demise."

Huffing a laugh, she relaxed her legs. "I'm sorry. I didn't mean to smother you. It just felt so good." Heat flooded her cheeks. "Thank you."

Placing one last reverent kiss on her mound, he shifted, looming over her before lowering to align their bodies. Brushing a kiss on her lips, he shook his head. "You never have to thank me for making you feel good. We're bonded now, and it's my honor to give you pleasure."

Languid from her orgasm, she tenderly stroked his face. "I want to please you too."

Gliding his hand down her body, his fingers searched, finding her core and rimming her wet opening. Gathering some of her essence, he spread it all over her deepest place. The tender motions jolted her heartbeat once more as arousal flared deep within.

"Nothing pleases me more than to know I'm going to claim this sweet, tight pussy as mine." His tone was possessive as his hand worked its magic on her core. "That I'll be the only one who ever touches your gorgeous body."

Her fangs pressed into her bottom lip as she grinned. "Unless I leave you once I save up my stipend," she teased, undulating against his fingers as he emitted a harsh laugh.

"Try it," he murmured, lowering his lips to hers. "Once I claim you, I'm never letting you go."

Wrapping her arms around his neck, she opened her legs wider, allowing him to settle deeper between her thighs. "Promise?"

Gripping the base of his cock, he touched his sensitive head to her drenched opening, hissing as he rested his forehead against hers. Dousing his cock with her slick honey, he gazed deep into her eyes.

Celine held on for dear life as he began to push inside, inch by slow inch, the possessive glint in his eyes deepening with every small thrust. "Promise," he whispered, drawing her into a tender kiss.

Celine's lips toyed with his as she adjusted to the feeling of having him *inside* her. It wasn't uncomfortable, but with every jut forward she felt fuller. The small spark of nervousness she'd felt when he entered the room returned, and she stiffened slightly beneath him.

"Don't tense up, darling," he whispered, drawing her into a kiss as his hand found her breast. His fingers toyed with her nipple, sending renewed sparks of pleasure through her body, and she uttered a soft groan.

"That's it," he said, his hips undulating against her as he began to work his thick cock in her tight channel. "Feel me as I pinch these tight little nipples and claim every part of you."

The dirty words sparked a thousand fires deep within, and she moaned his name.

"Yes, sweetheart, there you are…" He circled his hips, the motion causing the head of his shaft to brush a place deep within that caused her to gasp. Brown eyes lit with desire as he watched her, moving his hips to hit the spot once more.

"Is that it?" he asked, jutting against it in small, rapid thrusts as she speared her fingernails into the skin at his nape. "Oh yes," he said, his lips curving into a sexy grin as he continued the maddening motion. "How does that feel, sweetheart?"

"Full…and amazing…and…*ahh*…" Unable to finish, she closed her eyes, her head relaxing into the pillow as she absorbed each pleasure-filled thrust.

"My naughty little virgin," he murmured, lowering his mouth to her ear and rimming the shell with his tongue. "You love taking my cock, don't you?"

"Yes!" Gripping his shoulders, every last ounce of strength left her muscles as she opened herself to him.

"Goddess, Celine," he gritted, teeth clenched as the pace of his hips increased. "I've never felt anything so tight around me… You're like a vise…it feels so good, darling…"

A cry escaped her lips as happiness flooded her. She wanted so desperately to please him and felt immense joy he was experiencing pleasure too. Wanting to pull him deeper, she squeezed her inner muscles, reveling at his shout of pleasure as he jerked above her.

"Dirty girl," he rasped, lifting her leg and wrapping it around his waist, opening her even more. "You're squeezing me. Do it again."

Celine clenched her inner muscles, closing around him before releasing and clenching again. Bliss contorted every feature in his handsome face as he cried her name, and Celine had the fleeting thought that maybe, just maybe, she could still make him fall in love with her. If they shared such a deep connection physically, surely she could transpose that to an emotional connection.

"Look at me," he commanded, drawing her from the serious thoughts.

Staring into his eyes, she squeezed him everywhere she could—his shoulders, his cock, his waist—and clutched him as he neared the peak.

"I need you to come again," he said, lowering his hand between their bodies. Finding her clit, he rubbed concentric circles on the engorged nub as he fucked her. "Please, sweetheart, come with me. I need you—"

Aching to kiss him, she pulled him close, inhaling his words as she drew him into a passionate kiss. His deep groans of pleasure echoed in her mouth as she slid her tongue over his. His powerful body trembled against hers, the ministrations of his fingers on her clit driving her toward another cliff. Surrounded by his warm body and sultry moans, she dove off the side, headlong into another orgasm, as his body bucked against her.

He surged inside her, filling her one last time before his head snapped back. Screaming her name, he began to come, his body jerking above her as he erupted. Grunting with lust, his hips jolted with every hot, pulsing jet he shot into her body.

Craving every part of him, she wrapped her legs around his waist, pulling him close as the hurried jerks of his hips turned to smaller shudders. Filling her with one last pump, he collapsed, his body half-atop hers as he rested most of his weight on his side.

Giggling, she ran her calf over the back of his hairy thigh as he huffed against her neck.

"Now who's laughing?" he mumbled.

"I was just thinking how considerate you were to only collapse halfway over me so you don't crush me. Still the proper, polite aristocrat, even in bed."

Lifting his head, he nipped her lips before breaking into a wide grin. "We're both creatures of habit, aren't we?" Resting his head on his fist, he traced the sweaty skin between her breasts, causing her to shiver.

"Yes, but knowing is half the battle." Lifting her finger, she arched her eyebrows. "We can help each other lighten up. I'll make sure you don't drown in paperwork, and you can help me become more independent...or worldly...or whatever I need to be so people don't think I'm a boring dimwit."

"I want everyone to think you're as boring as drywall so no one will realize how magnificent you are," he teased, chucking her nose with his finger. "You're mine, and no one is allowed to look at you."

Pride swelled at his words. "It wouldn't matter if they did. I only want you, Sebastian."

"Thank the goddess," he whispered.

They lay entwined, gently caressing each other, as their bodies cooled. Eventually, he ran his thumb over her lip.

"Are you okay, darling? I wanted to be gentle your first time, but I might've gotten a bit carried away." He cocked a satiated eyebrow.

"I'm fine. It felt good once I got used to the fullness. And the spot you found..." Overcome with embarrassment, she flattened her lips.

"Yes?" he crooned, cupping her breast and running his thumb over her nipple. "Did you like it when I hit that spot, Celine?"

Biting the inside of her lip, she nodded.

"Good. I'll make sure to give it *lots* of attention every time we do this."

Taken with his sultry expression, she finally let the realization wash over her that they were bonded for eternity. Well, as long as they could figure out how to make each other happy. He had offered her the option to eventually leave if she saved up enough money, but she doubted she would ever wish to do so.

"What is it?"

"I was just thinking about the future. We didn't discuss this—although we should've—but I have an IUD. I have for years because it regulates my cycle. Since this happened so fast, I know we're not ready to discuss children, but I want to be honest with you."

Disappointment washed over his features as her heart fluttered. "Sebastian?"

He pasted on a smile, although it didn't quite reach his eyes. "We should've discussed it, and I'm sorry we didn't. It's been kind of a whirlwind few weeks." He lifted a sardonic brow.

"It has. I think we should allow ourselves to be newlyweds for a while and settle into this. We have eternity to discuss these things."

"My wise little aristocrat," he said, plopping a kiss on her lips. "That we do." Glancing down, he eyed their bodies as he began to slip. "Don't move. Be right back." Extricating from her embrace, he padded to the bathroom, wetting a cloth before returning to her. Urging her to lie on her back, he spread her legs, wiping away the evidence of their loving.

As he stroked her with the warm cloth, his eyes lit with sated desire. "I love seeing you covered in my release. Goddess, sweetheart, it's so sexy."

Shaken by his desire-laden words, she bit her lip, watching him through half-lidded eyes. Once finished, he tossed the cloth in the hamper and turned off the bedside light as she crawled under the covers. He slid beside her, drawing her close.

Sprawling over his broad body, she rested her cheek on his chest, splaying her palm over his heart as it beat firmly beneath it.

"Good night, my naughty little mate. You're officially no longer a virgin."

Grinning, she ran her palm over the spiky hairs on his chest. "I'm not naughty."

Laughter rumbled as he squeezed her. "Oh, darling, you might've convinced everyone else, but I've seen behind your curtain. Now be a good mate and let me sleep. You tired me out."

"Yes, sir," she said, cuddling into him as she yawned.

He responded with a slap on her butt, causing her to beam as she snuggled against him. Wrapped in her bonded mate's embrace, she closed her eyes and inhaled his musky scent as she gave way to her dreams.

Chapter 13

S ebastian dove headfirst into building a life with Celine, often berating himself for the centuries he'd wasted as a proclaimed bachelor. He quickly realized his feisty, precocious bonded mate was his perfect match, and he inwardly declared himself the biggest dolt on the planet for overlooking her for so long.

For one thing, she was exceedingly generous and polite to the interior design staff she'd hired to decorate the house. Every time Sebastian came home he would find her working alongside them, painting walls or hanging wallpaper. A wealthy aristocrat like Celine could've chosen to be pampered in luxury for the rest of her days. Instead, she was content to help, wanting to stamp her mark on the work. Sebastian admired her greatly for it, and he also thought her adorable when he discovered her in the worn work attire.

"Look at you," he said, two weeks after their bonding ceremony when he returned home for lunch. She was dressed in baggy overalls with paint splotches covering her perfect features. Running his finger over her paint-soaked cheek, he grinned. "Who would've guessed our proper Celine is an avid house painter?"

"Oh, stop it," she chided, swiping his chest. "I want to help, and it satisfies my urge to make things perfect." Gesturing around, her eyes lit with excitement. "Do you like the color?"

Surveying the living room, he admitted it was gorgeous. The deep forest green complimented the wood floor and stone fireplace, and he knew she would buy furniture that only enhanced the colors. Sliding his arm around her waist, he tugged her close, brushing a kiss on her lips. He ached to do more—perhaps spread some paint to other regions of her stunning body—but alas, they were surrounded by workers, so he behaved himself.

"I love the color. Well done."

"You're home for lunch again," she said, lifting to her toes to kiss him back. "I thought you always ate at the office."

"I find I can't go more than a few hours without seeing you, darling," he murmured, nipping her lips. "What do you think that means?"

Affection swam in her eyes as she smiled. "That you're slowly losing your desire to be a workaholic. It's a miracle."

Chuckling, he ran the backs of his fingers over her cheek. "Perhaps you've cured me. If so, I'm exceedingly thankful."

Her delight at his words was palpable, and he reveled in her stunning smile. In truth, Sebastian was becoming quite addicted to his mate, and he found himself longing for her when they were apart. Never in all his centuries on the planet had he craved the company of another, but now, he admitted he was hooked. He couldn't imagine building a future with anyone else, and he silently kicked himself for giving her an out. Would the day come when she saved up his monthly stipend and decided to leave? The dreary thought brought him great discomfort, so he pushed it away every time it appeared.

When she'd told him about her IUD, he'd experienced a moment of such melancholy his throat closed as he'd caressed her soft skin. He'd never given much thought to children, but now that he was with Celine he saw no reason to wait. She would be an excellent mother, and the possessive part of him wanted to bear a child with her. To create something special that belonged only to them. A child they could love and cherish as they continued to build their future.

Did she want that with him though? Or did she see bearing his child as another tie to him? Perhaps deep within, she still felt as if he'd bonded with her out of duty. Perhaps Sebastian had used that as an excuse, but deep down he knew the truth: each day, he was falling deeper into the abyss for his bonded mate.

Sebastian had never been in love before, but he had the stinging suspicion that it felt a lot like what he was experiencing. The need to be near her constantly. The bliss he felt when she tossed back her head and gave a joyful laugh. The bone-deep arousal he felt every time they made love. It was all-consuming, and he finally began to comprehend what Garridan had tried to explain about his feelings for Siora.

The emotion he felt for Celine was encompassing. Although that frightened him slightly, he also wanted to push through the fear to other side, knowing the reward of building a future with her would be so much more fulfilling than the staid, boring life he'd lived for so long.

After all this time, he craved a future with a mate and hoped he could convince her to stay. To bear his children and build a life full of affection and joy.

A s the weeks turned into months, Sebastian and Celine fell into an easy pattern. She focused on decorating the house while he performed his council duties. They attended the formal fetes and fundraisers together, Sebastian always so proud to have her on his arm.

One night, after a particularly stuffy fundraiser, they returned home and Celine proceeded to kick off her shoes in the foyer. Chuckling, Sebastian lifted her in his arms and carried her up the stairs.

"Why do you wear them if they hurt your feet, darling?" he asked, placing her on the bed and lowering beside her. Bringing her foot to his lap, he began to knead the swollen arch.

"Oh goddess..." she moaned, throwing her arm over her eyes as he massaged her foot. "That feels amazing." Squinting from under her arm, she gave a cheeky grin. "And I wear them because they're fashionable, of course. A prominent aristocratic council member must have an appropriately dressed female on his arm."

The corner of his lips curled. "I appreciate the sentiment, darling, but I prefer you without any clothes at all. I think you know that by now."

Heat flushed her cheeks as she bit her lip, adorable in the soft light of the bedside lamp. Rising, he slowly removed her dress, dragging it off her body along with her undergarments. Sebastian gazed at her, lust thrumming through his veins from her dewy skin as it glowed on the bed. Once he was naked, he straddled her, sliding his hands under her arms so her back rested against the headboard. After fluffing the pillows behind her to ensure she was comfortable, he balanced on his knees as he straddled her flushed body.

"Darling," he said, cupping her chin as his cock strained toward her. "I need to claim you here." He ran his thumb over her lips.

Doubt entered her eyes as her breaths grew heavy. "I don't know how. I don't want to do it wrong—"

A desire-laden laugh rushed from his lips. "Impossible," he whispered, inching toward her. "Just kiss me. I promise, anything you do to me feels good, sweetheart." He placed the sensitive tip of his cock on her lips, overwhelmed with how gorgeous she was as curiosity warred with doubt in her expression.

Finally, she took pity on him and opened those full lips. Seizing the moment, Sebastian slowly slipped inside.

Working his hips, he pumped into her wet mouth, overcome with how sexy she was as she stroked him with her lips and tongue. Those stunning ice-blue eyes locked with his, filled with desire and hope, and he chuckled as he caressed her cheek.

"It feels amazing. Just like that..." Increasing the pace of his hips, he fucked her sweet mouth, observing her confidence grow as she realized *she* was the one in control.

"Yes, darling," he rasped, placing his palms flat on the headboard to brace himself. She smiled around his cock, the little minx, causing the sensitive flesh to swell even more. "You have me in the palm of your hand. You always do. You know that, right?"

Lifting her hand to his sac, she gently squeezed as he groaned. Baring his fangs, he thought he might drown in the image of his sweet Celine sucking him as she caressed his most sensitive place.

"Naughty girl," he rasped, the base of his spine tingling as his climax loomed. "I smell your arousal. You're gushing as you suck me, aren't you, darling?"

She whimpered, nodding as she coated his shaft with her saliva.

Suddenly craving a deeper connection, he withdrew, sliding down her body and pushing her legs apart. Settling between her thighs, he thrust his hand in the hair at her nape, clutching as the sensitive head of his cock slipped through her essence.

"Open up to me, honey," he rasped, positioning himself at her core.

Wrapping her arms around him, she nodded. "I'm ready—"

Her back arched as he surged inside, claiming her as lust clouded his brain. Anchoring her by her hair, he thrust in strong, deep lunges, unable to control his need to possess her. Pressing his forehead to her neck, he inhaled her intoxicating scent as his hips worked her ravaged body. Aching to have all of her, he licked her neck, preparing it for his invasion.

"I need to drink from you, sweetheart," he rasped, overcome by the taste of her salty sweat on his tongue. Drinking from one's mate was a sacred tradition in Vampyre culture, and a threshold they hadn't yet crossed. "Please, Celine, I have to—"

"Yes," she cried, spearing her nails into his back. "Drink from me—"

Armed with her consent, he bared his fangs and thrust them deep into her vein. Her blood burst onto his tongue, coating it as he moaned. A thousand shards of pleasure shot to every cell in his frame as he consumed her, body and soul. Lost in her scent and spurred on by her sexy purrs, he fucked her, raw and deep, until she began to tremble.

"Oh yes...right there, Sebastian..." Her head fell lax on the pillow, baring her neck to him as her fingernails scraped his back. The little hellion was probably drawing blood, but Sebastian didn't care. All he could fathom was this moment, lost in his beautiful Celine as he loved her.

Closing his eyes, he emitted a deep groan, falling over the edge as the orgasm claimed him.

The walls of her tight pussy clenched, milking his release from his body as she shuddered below him. Locked inside her tight vise, he rode the wave, his lips still covering her pulsing vein as they experienced the high. His hips jerked, emptying the last of his release into her warm core, and he licked her neck, sealing her wounds with his self-healing saliva.

They lay entwined, sticky and sated, slowly caressing each other as they fell back to earth. She ran her nails over his scalp, the soft strokes infinitely pleasurable, and Sebastian felt the urge to say the three words he'd never said to another.

"I liked sucking you," she said, the words laced with a hint of shyness.

Lifting his head, he couldn't stop his sultry grin. "I liked it too."

"You did?"

Nodding, he caressed her jaw. "Darling, don't you know by now that I live for the moments you touch me? In any way, and for however long."

"My romantic Vampyre," she sighed, trailing her fingers over his back. "I never would've guessed."

Chuckling, he kissed her collarbone, understanding how special his romantic words were to her. Realization dawned that he needed to do more. Not just in the bedroom, but in their daily lives as well. Racking his brain, he tried to think of something that would show her. Not just with words or passionate lovemaking, but a real, tangible expression of how much she meant to him.

An idea slowly formed in his mind, and his lips curved as his wheels continued to spin.

"What's that mischievous grin for?" she asked, curiosity lacing her features.

"Nothing. I'm still high from being buried inside you, darling."

Biting her lip, she nodded. "Me too."

Feeling himself slip, he rose, cleaning them both before they crawled under the covers and held each other close. As she fell asleep in his arms, Sebastian stroked her hair, formulating the details of the gift he was going to give her. One that would show her he truly saw her, after all this time, and that there was no doubt his future belonged to her.

Chapter 14

Mila discovered Celine sitting underneath one of the oak trees in her expansive back yard. The branches offered shade from the sun, and she absently chewed her nail as her friend approached.

"No decorating today?" Mila asked, sitting on the spongy grass beside her.

"It's mostly finished," Celine said, staring off into the distance as she frowned. "I have a few small things left to decorate, but for the most part, the work is done."

"That's great. Why do you look miserable?"

Huffing a breath, she lifted her hands in an exasperated shrug. "Because after it's done, what the hell am I going to do?"

"Umm...I don't understand the question."

"I don't want to become a burden to Sebastian. Decorating the home has given me a purpose." She slowly trailed her palm over the grass. "Once it's done, am I just supposed to sit around all day and wait for him to come home? Won't that make me the simpering, useless female he always saw me as? What if he comes to resent me? Or worse, decides I'm the boring aristocrat everyone else thinks I am?"

"Wow," Mila said, leaning back on her palms. "There's a lot to unpack there." Pursing her lips, she contemplated. "First of all, I don't know why you're freaking out. Sebastian is clearly in love with you, Celine."

"Then why won't he say it?" she murmured, her lips forming a pout. "Sometimes, when we make love, I feel he's so close to saying it, but he never does."

"Have *you* said it? Sometimes men need a push, Celine. You know this better than most since your experience as *Anya* is what pushed him to finally acknowledge you."

Sighing, Celine's lips fluttered as she blew out a breath. "I'm afraid to say it first. Then he'll know he owns my heart." Staring at her friend, she almost choked on the emotion welling in her chest. "I don't want him to *own* me, Mila. I want us to be equals."

"Then tell him. He's not a mind reader, Celine."

"I know." Drawing her knees to her chest, Celine rested her chin upon them as she stared over the rolling hills. "I want to have his children...and build a family with him."

"Perhaps he wants that too. It's long past time you were a mother, Celine."

"But children will bind me to him even more. I don't want him to feel obligated to me."

"Well, you're bonded—"

"Yes, because my father forced it." Angrily shaking her head, she scowled. "But I want him to *choose* me. Is that too much to ask? Am I just being ridiculous?"

Sighing, Mila contemplated. "I don't know. He's not the most expressive man—"

"You should see him in the bedroom," Celine interjected, excitement lacing her tone. "Oh, Mila, he's so passionate—"

"Um, yeah, I'm all set." Mila held up her hand as Celine chuckled. "You two are still learning to communicate with each other, but now's not the time to hold back. You need to tell him what you want." Gazing into her eyes, her friend smiled. "Tell him you love him, Celine. I know you're afraid it will make him feel obligated to say it too, but maybe he's waiting for you. You won't know until you take the chance."

Tears burned Celine's eyes as she acknowledged Mila's words. "And what if he doesn't say it back?"

"Then you continue to save his monthly stipend and hope he gets his act together. If not, you'll always have the opportunity to leave down the road."

The thought of leaving Sebastian, whom she loved with every piece of her heart, was so distressing she pushed the possibility from her mind. "I can't accept that reality."

Rising, Mila wiped the grass off her backside before extending her hand. "Then make the reality you want, Celine. Come on—I need your help. I'm meeting a prospective new client at the coffee shop and want your opinion."

"Why do you need my opinion?" she asked, taking her hand and rising to her feet.

"Because, my dear," she said, waggling her brows, "I think I might want this one for myself. She plays for my team, if you know what I mean."

"Ohhhh," Celine said, clasping her hands under her chin. "I'd be honored to help you assess. Let me wash up, and I'll walk to town with you."

Hoping she could help her friend find love, Celine tucked her words deep inside, praying she could gather the strength to face her bonded mate and voice her true feelings.

Chapter 15

A week later, Celine finally summoned the courage to confront Sebastian. He'd seemed a bit distracted lately, sometimes rushing off to take important calls at odd hours of the day and night, and she was worried he'd begin to focus on work again now that they'd settled into their lives. She'd decided she would tell him she wanted to remove her IUD and start trying to get pregnant, hoping that would keep him focused on things at home now that the renovation was mostly finished.

When he breezed through the front door, Celine's heart leaped in her chest as she flitted around the kitchen putting the finishing touches on everything she'd prepared. He stepped into the room and broke into a wide grin.

"What's all this?" he asked, striding toward her and drawing her into a deep kiss. "Did you prepare lunch for me, darling?"

"Yes," she said, gesturing to the island countertop. "I prepared some Slayer blood and some food too. You've been working so hard lately I figured you deserved a treat."

"Have you been keeping tabs on me, dear?" Leaning down, he brushed the tip of his nose against hers.

"Well, you've just seemed a bit distracted with all the work calls..." She drifted off, not wanting to complain. "But I know your job is important. Our people are lucky to have you."

A tender expression crossed his features, and he nodded. "My work is important, but nothing is more important than you, Celine. You know that, right?"

Hating the tears that welled in her eyes, she worked her jaw, struggling to speak. "I...honestly, I don't know, Sebastian. I think we're still learning to communicate, and sometimes I'm not sure what to think."

His lips formed a sympathetic smile. "We are, and I appreciate how patient you've been with me." His fingers stroked her jaw as he spoke, his tone reverent. "I was a grumpy, lovelorn bachelor for way too long and never learned how to be romantic."

"I think you're doing a fine job."

Chuckling, he shook his head. "In some areas, perhaps..."—his eyes lit with desire—"but I know I could do more. In fact, I have something to show you." Stepping back, he extended his hand.

Curious, she placed her palm in his, following him as he tugged her toward the back door. He led her outside, past the tree where she'd had the discussion with Mila, and through a thicket of dense trees and brush. Eventually, they made it to a clearing with an expansive meadow that housed a large circular wooden fence.

"Garridan never used this piece of land, but it's part of the property, and I've finally commissioned it for use."

"Oh," she said, surveying the field. "What for?"

"As you can see, the workers I hired already built the horse corral." Pointing toward the side of the corral, he grinned. "And the stable can go there if that works for you."

Celine's heart began to pound as she struggled to comprehend what he was saying. "If you're building stables, you don't need my approval."

"Well, darling, since the stables are for you, I would rather have your opinion."

"For me?" she whispered.

"Yes, sweetheart." Encircling her wrists, he brought them to his chest. "I racked my brain to find something that would show you how much I love you, Celine, and that I *see* you. I remember you telling me you wanted that when you first turned my life upside down." He flashed a teasing grin. "I'm building you a stable, darling, where you can open an academy and train children to ride horses. My dear, you can muck out as many stalls as your heart desires."

A laugh escaped her throat as she spread her palms over his pecs. "You're building me a stable?"

"Yes. And the academy will be yours to run however you wish. It will allow you to build your own business so you're not so dependent on me." Leaning down, he nudged her nose with his. "I know you want your independence, Celine, and I have no wish to deny you that. I just want you to be happy. It's the only chance we have of building the future we want."

Tears ran down her cheeks as she stood frozen, awed by the immensely romantic gesture. Unable to form words, her arms snaked around his neck, and he drew her into a warm embrace.

"Don't cry, sweetheart," he crooned, soothing her as he rubbed her back. "This was supposed to make you smile."

"I'm overwhelmed," she said, drawing back to gaze into his eyes. "I wished for so long you'd love me back, but I wasn't sure you would ever see me as more than a burden forced on you by my father."

"A burden?" he asked, stroking her hair. "Goddess, Celine, you're the best damn thing that's ever happened to me. I was a shell of a man buried in work when you shook up my world. I'm so thankful for you, darling." Leaning forward, he rested his lips against her ear. "And you're so deliciously dirty in bed, my naughty little virgin."

Her cheeks reddened with embarrassment as she swatted his chest. "I'm not naughty, and I'm certainly no longer a virgin. You took care of that quite promptly after we bonded."

Tossing back his head, he laughed. "I certainly did, but you are delectably naughty, Celine. It's one of my favorite things about you."

"Sebastian," she whispered, tenderly stroking his face. "I love you so much. I've loved you for centuries. I'm so honored you finally decided to love me back. I want to give you babies and build a future with you if you want the same."

Cocking a brow, he murmured, "I'll agree on one condition. You *must* teach our children how to muck out stalls. I think I'll enjoy watching that very much."

"You devil," she chided, biting her lip. "Will you ever stop teasing me?"

"Never." He brushed a kiss over her lips. "How can I when it's so fun? Your cheeks turn the sexiest shade of red when I tease you, darling—"

Done with his tender chiding, she drew him close, cementing her lips to his as they shared a torrid kiss. Sebastian groaned, pressing his body to hers as their tongues glided over each other's, sending sparks of desire through her veins.

Gently breaking the kiss, she pressed her forehead to his. "Thank you for this." She glanced out over the meadow. "My own business where I can teach children and work with horses. It's a dream I never imagined would come true for someone like me, raised to be a boring aristocrat."

"'Boring' isn't even in my vocabulary when it comes to you." Gliding a hand over her hair, his eyes darted between hers. "I love you, Celine. Thank you for being patient with me."

"I love you," she cried, rising to her toes to peck his lips. "Thank you for seeing who I truly am."

Lowering, he swept her into his arms and began to carry her home. As he plodded across the yard, she rested her head on his chest, closing her eyes and thanking Etherya for her gorgeous, thoughtful mate.

Once they crossed the threshold of the back door, he set her on her feet and locked the door.

Glancing at the counter, her lips formed a sultry smile. "I have a feeling we're not going to be eating lunch for a while."

Hunger entered his gaze as he slowly approached. "Oh, I intend to feast...just not on the delicious spread you prepared..."

Arousal flared within as her mate approached, reaching for her with his broad, talented hands as she squealed. Rapt with joy, she pivoted, running from the room and bolting up the stairs.

His deep laugh followed as he trailed after her. "You know I'll have to punish you for running, right, darling?"

Throwing herself on the bed, she waited for her lover to arrive. He slowly approached, gazing at her with such adoration her heart threatened to explode in her chest. Extending her arms, she beckoned to him. Strong, stoic Sebastian, the only man she'd ever loved, and the man who finally loved her exactly as she was.

Enfolding him in her arms, she opened every last piece of her heart. Her skillful, soulful Vampyre loved her, slowly and passionately, whispering tender words as they cemented the future they would build for centuries to come.

Before You Go

Well, dear readers, Celine and Sebastian found their happy ending! I think Mila needs to find hers too. What do *you* think? Make sure to check out all of my books at **RebeccaHefner.com** and thank you for reading!

Did you know that Rebecca has an online store where she sells **signed books**, an Etherya's Earth **adult coloring book**, and more? Check out her website for more info!

Acknowledgments

Thanks to everyone who asked for Celine and Sebastian's story!

Thanks to Megan, Bryony, Anthony and Sarah for being part of my team and for making my books shine.

And thanks to every one of you who reads my books!

About the Author

USA Today bestselling author Rebecca Hefner grew up in Western NC and now calls the Hudson River of NYC home. In her youth, she would sneak into her mother's bedroom and read the romance novels stashed on the bookshelf, cementing her love of HEAs. A huge Buffy and Star Wars fan, she loves an epic fantasy and a surprise twist (Luke, he IS your father).

Before becoming an author, Rebecca had a successful twelve-year medical device sales career. After launching her own indie publishing company, she is now a full-time author who loves writing strong, complex characters who find their HEAs.

Rebecca can usually be found making dorky and/or embarrassing posts on TikTok and Instagram. Please join her so you can laugh along with her!